THE
Phantom
Isles

STEPHEN ALTER

THE
Phantom
Isles

BLOOMSBURY
CHILDREN'S
BOOKS

Text copyright © 2007 by Stephen Alter
Chapter opener illustrations copyright © 2007 by Jonathan Bean
Face illustrations copyright © 2007 by John Rocco

Published by Bloomsbury U.S.A. Children's Books
175 Fifth Avenue, New York, NY 10010
Distributed to the trade by Holtzbrinck Publishers

Library of Congress Cataloging-in-Publication Data
Alter, Stephen.
The phantom isles / by Stephen Alter. — 1st U.S. ed.
p.   cm.
Summary: Three friends and the librarian in a Massachusetts town must help
each other to free the ghosts that have been imprisoned in books by a professor
on a fantastical island many years ago.
ISBN-13: 978-1-58234-738-7 • ISBN-10: 1-58234-738-7
[1. Ghosts—Fiction. 2. Books—Fiction. 3. Supernatural—Fiction.] I. Title.
PZ7.A46373Ph 2007   [Fic]—dc22   2006013196

First U.S. Edition 2007
Typeset by Westchester Book Composition
Printed in the U.S.A. by Quebec World Fairfield

1 3 5 7 9 10 8 6 4 2

For Pete and Nathu

Seabirds on the wing and wings on a conch,
The spell reversed and the curse unspelled . . .
Arora 'rora 'rora
A 'ror a 'ror arora
No one knows when the lost spirits will come home,
Their secret is written on the star-catchers' scrolls

—FROM A FOLK SONG OF ILHAS DOS FANTASMAS

THE Phantom Isles

1

Courtney, Orion, and Ming crawled through the rotting mulch and ducked beneath a tangled hedge of rhododendrons. In the darkness the wet leaves and limp blossoms licked their arms and faces. The dank smells of moldering foliage, dying flowers, and decaying bark added to the uncomfortable sensations of bugs crawling up their ankles and spiderwebs in their hair. Earlier that night there had been a thunderstorm. Though the rain had stopped, the air was warm and humid, as if a huge invisible dog were breathing down their necks.

The clouds had pulled apart to reveal a sliver of the moon, hanging above them in the sky like a sharpened sickle. Fifty feet ahead, they could see the profile of the library with its granite walls, cast-iron grilles, and turreted roof that made it look like a fortress.

"Somebody's there," whispered Orion.

"No, that's just a security light," said Courtney. "It's always on."

"How do we get inside?" Ming asked.

"Follow me." Courtney lifted herself off her knees and into a crouch. The three of them crossed the empty parking lot and ran through the shadows of an overhanging oak until they reached a corner of the library, where they huddled together, listening for sounds.

"Are you sure there isn't a burglar alarm?" said Ming, pressing herself against the rough stone wall.

"No, of course there isn't," said Courtney, who always had an answer even if she wasn't sure. "Nobody's going to steal old books."

In the distance they heard a car and saw its headlights flickering through the trees along Elm Street. After the sound of its engine faded into the distant mumble of the interstate, Courtney led them along the wall to a barred window at ground level.

"Come on, help me," she said. Together, the three of them were able to lift the heavy metal grate. Once this had been removed, Courtney pushed on the window, which swung open easily. Earlier that day, she had unlatched it from inside.

"Ming, you're the smallest, you go first. There's a desk right under the window."

Hesitating for a moment, Ming felt Orion push her forward. It was like crawling into a mailbox. She squirmed in backward and feet first. Her arms scraped against the windowsill and she felt herself begin to fall, but at the last second her shoe kicked the desk, and she was able to stand up before lowering herself to the floor. Inside the library basement it was completely dark, like a cave or a tomb. Above her, Ming could just make out Orion's shape as he slid through the window and nearly fell on top of her. Every scuffling sound they made was amplified. Courtney followed, and the window closed behind her with a thud.

"Where's the flashlight?"

"Here," said Orion.

A feeble beam of yellow light poked through the darkness, and they could see one another's faces in the glow.

"It isn't very bright," said Ming. "You should have got new batteries."

Orion shone the light over the rows of stacks that lined the basement. The gray metal shelves reached almost to the roof, and the spines of books stood in ordered ranks. All three of them had been in the library basement many times before, but it looked different in the dark, as if everything were closer together. The musty odors of paper, ink, and glue were suffocating, and there was a muffled silence in the stacks, as if all of the words in all those books had never once been uttered aloud.

Now that they were inside, Ming led the way, reading out the call numbers on the stacks as Orion's flashlight wavered from shelf to shelf.

"Here we go," said Ming, stopping in front of a sign that read BF250-GH85. She made her way down the rows of books until her fingers came to rest on one.

"BF1612.C76," she whispered. It was an ordinary-looking book, old and heavy as a brick, with a plain green cover that had no words or decoration—the kind of book that seemed to have been buried in the library forever, like a forgotten fossil.

Courtney leaned closer as Orion held the flashlight steady. The first few pages were blank, and on one of these was a smudged stamp in red ink:

As Ming turned to the title page, the batteries in the flashlight started to grow dimmer, though they could still read the words:

THE COMPLEAT NECROMANCER
An Investigation into the
Mysteries of the Afterlife
by
Prof. Hezekiah T. Osgood
1946

"What's a necromancer?" Orion whispered.

"Someone who talks to ghosts," said Courtney.

At the top of the page was a strange-looking symbol, a conch shell with wings.

"Quickly, page two hundred and three," said Ming.

"What time is it?" asked Courtney.

"Almost midnight." Orion glanced over his shoulder.

Ming flipped ahead, the pages brittle and sticking together.

Her fingers trembled, and the old volume suddenly felt heavier. Two days before, when Ming had discovered the book, it had fallen open to page 203, but tonight it seemed as if she would never find what she was looking for, as if the numbers had all been scrambled and everything was out of place.

"There it is," said Orion, shaking the flashlight to try to make it brighter.

" 'Spells and Incantations for Summoning the Deceased,' " Courtney read the chapter title under her breath.

"Are you sure you want to do this?" Orion asked.

"You're afraid," said Courtney.

"No, I'm not."

"It says we have to read it all together," said Ming. " 'Three friends must gather in the darkness and conspire to raise the dead. If their voices join in unison, these words expelled in a single breath, only then will the spirits be revealed.' "

"What do we have to say?" Orion asked.

Ming pointed to the verses at the center of the page.

Nore glamat nantam algeron
Mutae crop gnong porce atum
Nor denam lostat sol manedron
Mutan ebel uknyn kul ebenatum

Gni loti velulu levi toling
Na pizrah tolo tharzipan
Gnilor ports ninstrop roling
Na pizro lodab abado lorzipan

"What does it mean?" Courtney wondered aloud.

"The book doesn't say," said Ming.

"How are we supposed to pronounce the words?" Orion said, trying to decipher the jumbled letters.

"We'll just have to do the best we can," Ming said. "Hurry, before the flashlight goes out."

"I can hardly read it," Orion complained, leaning forward nervously.

"Remember, all in one breath," said Courtney. "Here we go—one, two, three . . ."

It was like taking a big gulp of air before you jump into the deep end of a swimming pool. As they read the words aloud, their voices sounded strange and distant. At first the syllables seemed to fit together awkwardly, and they had to squint to read the tiny print, but by the second stanza it felt as if they were all speaking the same language. The rhyme and rhythm fell together. In the hollow darkness of the library basement, their three voices became the echo of a single voice that rustled the pages on the book like the first breeze before a storm.

After they had finished, none of them moved, eyes fixed on the page, where the words seemed garbled now, as if the ink had started to run and blur. But it was just the fading flashlight, which had grown dimmer and dimmer until it finally went out. Orion shook it again, but the batteries were now completely dead, and darkness closed in around them.

"Let's get out of here," said Ming.

"Wait," said Orion. "Listen."

They held their breath for almost a minute.

"It's nothing," said Courtney. "The spell didn't work."

"Did you really think it would?" said Orion.

"No, of course not." Courtney laughed nervously. "I don't believe in ghosts."

"Especially not in libraries," said Ming, trying to sound relieved.

"Okay, let's go," said Orion.

"Wait, I have to put the book back on the shelf, but I can't see." Ming was fumbling about in the dark, her hands brushing the cold metal shelves.

All three of them reached out and felt along the stacks, trying to locate the empty space where the book had been. Eventually, Ming found a gap and pushed the volume into place. Stumbling over one another, they made their way back down the row of shelves.

"We could turn on a light," said Ming.

"Don't be stupid," said Courtney. "Somebody might see it and call the cops."

"Ouch," said Orion, as he bumped into the desk.

Through the squares of glass in the window above, the moon peered in on them. It seemed much larger now, like a giant eye, half-opening out of sleep.

Climbing onto the desk, Courtney reached up and struggled with the latch before prying it loose. Though climbing inside had been easy, it was going to be much harder to get out.

"You'll have to boost me," said Courtney. "Then I can help pull each of you up."

She was about four inches taller than the other two. Having grown a lot this year, Courtney was self-conscious about her height, though at times like this it was an advantage. With all three of them standing on the desk, it began to creak as if the legs were going to break. Finally, Orion and Ming were able to lift Courtney high enough so that she could scramble through. After that she dragged Ming up while Orion pushed from below. Now he was left alone in the basement. While the two girls reached down to help him, he tried to scale the wall.

Just then they heard a siren.

Courtney and Ming let go of Orion's wrists. He stood on the desk as the wailing of the siren grew louder. Even inside the basement the sound seemed to be coming in his direction. Outside, the girls kneeled next to the window, trying to decide if they should run and hide. There was more than one siren now, and they could see red and blue lights flashing along Elm Street. A fire truck went by, followed by an ambulance, but instead of turning down the street toward the library, the sirens kept on going in the opposite direction.

Ming could feel her heart pounding in her throat, and her mouth had gone dry. Courtney let out her breath and turned back toward the window.

"Orion!" she whispered. "Come on. Let's get you out of there. Orion?"

"Orion!"

There was no reply.

2

Earlier, when Ming had first found *The Compleat Necromancer*, she read the introduction, which described a country called Ilhas dos Fantasmas. This was where Hezekiah Osgood, the author, had done his research on ghosts. Ming had never heard of the place before, but after checking upstairs in the reference section of the library, she came upon an entry in the *Encyclopedia Orientalia*, which explained that the Republic of Ilhas dos Fantasmas (also known as Prithvideep) lies in the middle of the Indian Ocean, just south of the equator. The golden sands of these remote islands are washed by the Bromeil current, a seasonal swirl of water that circles up from Antarctica, carrying with it a multitude of squid, krill, and plankton. As sailors have known for centuries, the current is especially treacherous in early August, bearing many ships to their doom on the coral reefs that ring Ilhas dos Fantasmas.

A chain of six islands, all but one of which is forested, make up the smallest nation on Earth. It has a combined landmass of thirty-two square kilometers and a total population of 923. The inhabitants of Prithvideep trace their ancestry to a mix of cast-aways, wanderers, and seafarers from every continent in the world, who have settled there over the past three centuries. In 1719, the Portuguese laid claim to the islands and gave them their name. However, Lisbon never asserted its rule or appointed a governor, for the territory was so minuscule it could hardly be considered a colony. At that time the population was no more than thirty, all but eight of whom belonged to the same family. The patriarch was Prithvi Sangarajan, a fisherman from the Malabar coast, who was lost at sea during a monsoon storm and suddenly found himself riding the Bromeil current to another destiny. His future wife, Philomenia, arrived six months later. Her story has never been fully explained, though it is whispered that she was the mistress of a pirate from Zanzibar who threw her overboard in a drunken quarrel. There is another version, recounted within the family, that Philomenia was the daughter of a Spanish admiral, and the sole survivor of a wreck that sank his galleon. Whatever the truth may be, the Prithvis have always been the first family of Ilhas dos Fantasmas, and many of the inhabitants can trace part of their lineage back to Sangarajan and Philomenia.

As Ming continued reading, she learned that Ilhas dos Fantasmas got its name from early lore and legends about ghosts that are believed to have once haunted the islands, though there seems to be no current evidence of phantoms. According to some accounts, these spirits, known as *arora*[1] in the local dialect, once lived side

---

1. *Arora* is an expression used only on Ilhas dos Fantasmas, but it shares the same root as the English word *aurora*. Like many other words in the island's language, it is a local variation of the European spelling.

by side with human beings until they suddenly disappeared, never to be seen again. This is one of the many mysteries and marvels of these islands. Another is a unique form of astrology practiced by men known as star-catchers.[2]

Until recently, the people of Ilhas dos Fantasmas used only feather money. Though there are no native birds on the islands, many migratory species pass through Prithvideep, crossing the equator in either direction. Before the introduction of modern currency, islanders collected feathers and considered these a form of wealth.

When Prithvideep declared independence from Portugal in 1912, nobody outside the islands really noticed. A constitution was drawn up, with a few unusual innovations, including a provision that the elected president of the Republic serve for a fixed term of seven years, after which he or she is sacrificed to the sharks.[3] This political ritual was decried by the few outside observers who visited the islands, and it attracted some attention in America, when whaling vessels returned with stories of distant lands. The Learned Society for the Elucidation of Primitive Cultures, based in Hornswoggle, Massachusetts, decided to send a scholar to Prithvideep in 1914 to learn more about the islands and help foster puritan values and democratic ideals. Professor

---

2. Using the photosensitive properties of a rare gum tree (*Glutinous luminosa*), found only on these islands, the star-catchers produce strips of bark cloth that are spread on the beach at night. The light from distant galaxies and constellations leaves its mark on the surface of these scrolls, much like images on a camera film. By reading the curved shapes and patterns that are preserved, star-catchers can predict the future.

3. This practice was stopped in 1973, though there are occasional agitations to resurrect the tradition depending on who is president.

Hezekiah T. Osgood, his wife, Clara, and their son, Nicodemus, who was only six months old, were sent by whaling ship. The Bromiel current, full of squid and plankton, attracted many whales and whaling vessels from America. Six weeks after leaving Hornswoggle, the Osgoods found themselves in a dinghy, paddling through the waves and across the reef to the shores of the largest island of Prithvideep.

Their arrival was uneventful, though Hezekiah had loaded his musket just in case. Two of the islanders helped drag the dinghy ashore and led the Osgoods to a grove of coconut palms where the president of the Republic was taking his afternoon nap in a hammock. He still had four more years left in his term and slept soundly. When finally awakened, he decreed that the Americans could build themselves a home at one end of the coconut grove, so long as they promised not to cut any of the trees. All of this was communicated in hand gestures and signs. One of the first things Hezekiah did, after building his thatch hut, was to begin studying the language, and he soon discovered it was a combination of all the different vernaculars represented on the island. The Americans had little influence on Prithvideep, despite Hezekiah's establishing a Latin grammar academy—which closed down soon after it started—and Clara's futile efforts to get the women to wear bonnets. On the other hand, the effects of Prithvideep on the Osgoods were considerably more profound.

3

A hundred years ago, on a bright May morning, after the tide has retreated, a young boy named Porquoix swims out to the reef. He carries a light harpoon with which he plans to skewer an octopus for lunch. The water is almost as clear as the air, and the fluttering waves break along the rim of the lagoon like the ruffled white hem on the blue pinafore that Porquoix's mother is wearing today. She watches from the door of their bungalow as her son swims steadily out to sea.

When he reaches the reef, Porquoix stands up and waves to his mother. The water is ankle deep, and he can see the bright colors of fish and coral. He knows every inch of the reef and has fished here for almost as long as he has been able to swim. The boy is thirteen, and like all of the children born on Ilhas dos Fantasmas, he has a tattoo on his left cheek, the symbol of a winged conch shell. Tightening the strap on his goggles, Porquoix wades along the reef until he comes to a narrow trench. The water here is a darker shade of blue and drops away between the coral cliffs. Taking a deep breath and holding his harpoon tight, Porquoix dives into the trench. As he swims down through the water, leaving a trail of bubbles, he can see the coral more clearly now. Bright orange and yellow tendrils wave around him while green parrot fish swim just out of reach. The reef wall descends over a hundred feet, and the trench is like a crooked gash filled with fish and eels, lobsters and sea urchins. A huge manta ray lifts off the ocean floor and swims away like a drifting shadow. Porquoix sees it out of the corner of his eye, but his attention is fixed on a cave, its mouth rimmed with purple coral. He is now twenty feet below the surface, and his ears pop as he swims toward the cave. Inside, he knows there is an octopus, hiding in the fluid darkness. Porquoix peers into the crevice, trying to make out the shapes within the shadows. He sees tentacles begin to move, like fingers curling into a fist. Drawing back the harpoon, he gets ready to spear the octopus. In his mind, he can already see his mother cooking it on a spit. But at that moment, just when he is about to plunge the harpoon into the cave, a shark comes by and takes the young fisherman for its lunch.

Porquoix feels no pain, only a dull crunch around his ribs and a sensation of relief, like peeling off wet clothes after you've been caught in a downpour. He isn't in the ocean any longer but in a place he's never seen before, a spiral chamber with curving walls. This tunnel is suffused with light, but there seems to be no source of illumination—no candles or lanterns. Somewhere in the distance, Porquoix can hear a curious sound, faint and musical, like the plaintive cry of a bird. There is a strange smell too, like ammonia and burning chocolate, sharp and sweet at the same time. He looks down at his hand, which no longer holds the harpoon, and he can see there are no lines on his palm or prints on his fingers. Instead, the skin is as smooth and white as the flesh of a coconut. Though he realizes that he is no longer alive, Porquoix isn't afraid. He can think and hear and smell and see, but it feels as if he has shed a part of himself, the outer layers of his skin. For a brief moment, he thinks of his mother standing in the doorway of their bungalow, wearing her blue apron fringed with white lace. The boy feels a passing sadness, but not strong enough to make him weep. He closes his eyes as the image melts away.

Porquoix begins to walk. Instead of the rough sand or the brittle texture of the coral reef, the ground beneath him feels smooth and polished. His bare feet, which moments before had been kicking in the salt water, now carry him down the curving length of the chamber. He feels as if he is running, but he does not need to take a single breath, no exertion in his limbs. Porquoix tries to slow his stride, but he is being pulled toward a point in the distance that he still can't see. The light is changing now, growing brighter, with an amber hue that seems warmer and more comforting. By now the music has grown louder too, and more distinct, each note punctuating the silence with the clarity of a silver bell. The ringing tones have a metallic sharpness but are strangely soothing, like the steady tapping of a jeweler's hammer.

4

Alma Parker unlocked the doors of the Carville Public Library at nine o'clock each weekday morning. She was a short, efficient-looking woman with dark brown hair who had been the head librarian for the past eight years. Alma was proud of the fact that she never missed a day of work. The only time she had arrived late to open the library was during a blizzard three years ago when even the snowplows had trouble making it down the street.

The library stood on a hill overlooking Hornswoggle Bay and the lighthouse, which was built on a rocky promontory, connected to the mainland by a seawall. Alma had lived in the town all her life, but the view of the bay and the lighthouse always made her stop for a moment and catch her breath.

Picking up the newspapers at the front door, Alma took these inside and arranged them on the rack. Then she checked the book return, which was empty, and adjusted the date on the rubber stamp at the checkout desk. Most days, nobody showed up until nine thirty, which gave her enough time to turn on all the lights and set the coffee brewing in her office.

This morning, everything seemed to be just the same as it always was. The thunderstorm from the night before had passed and the morning was clear and fresh after the rain. While the library had a gloomy, musty atmosphere—it had been built over 120 years ago—Alma had done her best to brighten things up with posters on the walls and colorful book displays. The town of Carville was always short of money, but she had persuaded the selectmen to let her repaint the library last year. The lemon yellow she chose for the walls made everything look more cheerful, despite the murky brown carpets underfoot and the dark wooden beams overhead.

The only part of the library that Alma hadn't been able to redecorate were the stacks. Each morning when the librarian went downstairs to turn on the lights, she wondered how to make it more inviting—by adding vases of artificial flowers? Painting the shelves light blue? Or opening up a space with chairs and lamps for reading? But there was really nothing she could do that would have made the stacks less claustrophobic and depressing. A curving staircase descended into the basement, where most of the books were kept because there wasn't enough room upstairs. Alma sometimes joked that it was like a dungeon where all of these volumes were imprisoned, just waiting to be released.

As she pressed the main switch, a line of fluorescent bulbs flickered on and a stark white glow lit up the central aisle between the stacks. At this point, Alma usually returned upstairs, but today she had a premonition that something wasn't quite right, an uneasy feeling that made her walk between the rows of shelves.

When she got to the end, she saw a desk out of place. Looking up, she noticed that the window was unlatched. Glancing at her feet, she caught sight of a flashlight lying on the floor.

Alma was a sensible, levelheaded woman who seldom got alarmed. But seeing the obvious signs of an intruder, she began to feel unsettled. Turning around, she looked to either side and slowly began to make her way back down the aisle, peering into each row of stacks. There was hardly any place to hide in the basement. When she reached the stairs, Alma was about to go back up to her office and call the police, but something made her hesitate. There wasn't a sound or any sign of movement. The stacks lay silent and still as a catacomb.

Walking down the aisle again, she looked more closely at the rows upon rows of books, feeling an unfamiliar presence in the room. A rational person by nature, the librarian told herself that she was imagining things. Whoever had broken into the stacks the night before must have already left. Then she came to the row marked BF250-GH85. At the far end, she could see a book lying on the floor. Hesitating, Alma went forward and picked it up.

A Comprehensive History of American Whaling Vessels.

Turning the book over in her hands, she read the call number, then looked up to see where it belonged on the shelf. The regimented spines of books arrayed in front of her seemed strangely forbidding. She realized the book that she'd picked up belonged in a different section altogether. With the practiced eyes of a librarian, Alma also noticed another book that had been put on the shelf upside down. It was an old, bricklike tome with a drab green cover. She pulled it out and replaced it right side up.

Returning to the center aisle, where the light was brighter, the librarian opened the whaling book in her hands. The first thing she noticed was an ornate bookplate pasted on the inside of the front cover. It had a line drawing of three palm trees, an old-fashioned inkstand with a quill pen, and a winged conch shell. The inscription read:

 This book is donated
to the Carville Public Library
from the personal collection of
Prof. Hezekiah T. Osgood
by his son
Nicodemus J. Osgood
1984

Alma was familiar with the bookplate. Quite a few of the older volumes in the library had come from the Osgood collection. They had been cataloged and dispersed throughout the stacks. Most of these were obscure books that nobody checked out. Turning the page, Alma found the familiar signature as well, a neat but spidery hand that spelled out the former owner's name. Prof. Hezekiah Osgood had returned to Massachusetts after years of research in the East. By the time he came back to Hornswoggle in 1933, the town had been renamed Carville. Professor Osgood died at the age of 103, having outlived his wife, Clara, by thirty years. Alma remembered seeing him when she was a child, a stooped old man who walked his spaniels along the waterfront. She had also heard rumors about the Osgoods, but the librarian considered these stories to be nothing more than superstitious gossip, and she didn't like to think ill of the dead. Besides, the Osgoods were among the most generous benefactors of the library, and there was a brass plaque on the wall upstairs that recognized their contributions.

She was about to close the book and return it to its proper place on the shelf when something made her cry out. Alma had never screamed in her life, and certainly not in the library, but this was the loudest, most frightened sound she had ever made.

Between the pages of the book, she saw the profile of a boy's face. The words were still there, printed on the paper, but hovering just above them, like a filmy, translucent layer, was an unmistakable image, as if traced in the air. Later, when Alma tried to explain it to herself, she thought the face reminded her of a watermark that seemed to be part of the paper but also lifted off the page. The boy's features were completely lifelike, and she could see the freckles on his nose and the tattoo on his cheek. Unlike a photograph, the image moved and the face turned to look at her. His eyes were a distant gray color, like smoke, and Alma felt certain that he could see her too. The boy looked almost as startled as the librarian. For a moment it seemed as if he would also cry out, though he remained silent.

Slowly, in the quivering light of the fluorescent bulbs, the image began to shift like a reflection on a fluid surface. The boy's face seemed to lean forward, as if peering through a window. He looked as if he had been swimming, his hair wet and tousled. Around his neck, Alma noticed a pair of old-fashioned goggles. Finally, the rising panic in her mind sent a delayed signal to her hands, and she slammed the book shut. Like a candle flame that has been snuffed out, the apparition disappeared.

5

But what about Orion?

He was okay. The night before, when the sirens started, Orion had panicked and jumped down from the desk. Running back into the stacks, he had tried to hide but got lost in the maze of shelves. A few minutes later, hearing Courtney and Ming calling, he headed in the wrong direction, feeling his way blindly through the dark. Eventually, though, he was able to get back to the window. His two friends had hauled him up, gasping for breath like someone who has almost drowned. It was only later, when they were heading back home, that Orion realized he had dropped his flashlight, but by then it was too late.

Now he was sitting in the sixth-grade homeroom listening to Mrs. Hokum give instructions about their final projects in social studies. Ming, whose desk was next to his, leaned over and whispered.

"Did you hear? Courtney got caught last night. Her mother woke up while she was sneaking back into her room. She's been grounded for a month."

"She didn't tell on us, did she?" said Orion, trying not to move his lips so the teacher wouldn't notice.

"No, she swears she didn't," said Ming.

Though Courtney was in seventh grade, she was only a few months older than Ming and Orion. The three of them lived near one another and always got together during lunch and after school.

"My parents will kill me if they find out," said Orion. "I left my flashlight at the library."

"We can go back this afternoon and look for it."

"I don't know if we should. . . ."

"Orion!" Mrs. Hokum's voice went up an octave.

He looked at the teacher and sat up straight.

"If you've got something important to say, why don't you tell the rest of us?"

"Sorry, Mrs. Hokum. It's nothing."

"Well then, Ming?" the teacher continued, advancing toward them. "Have you got something to share with the class?"

Ming shook her head, then quickly put a hand over her mouth to hide a nervous smile.

"As both of you know, I don't stand up here and talk just to hear myself speak," said Mrs. Hokum. "And I don't like others interrupting me."

Ming could see Marigold Deitz smirking in the front row. She was one of the more popular girls in the class who looked down her nose at everyone else.

"Sorry, Mrs. Hokum," said Ming.

"If I hear any more whispering, you'll both spend lunchtime in here vacuuming the floors."

Mrs. Hokum was the worst teacher at Carville Middle School.

Everybody knew this, except for the principal, Mr. Abernathy, who praised her for having the neatest bulletin boards and keeping her desks in line. Though Mrs. Hokum claimed otherwise, the only reason she talked was to hear herself speak, and her voice had a nasal monotone that sounded like a wasp buzzing against a screen, annoying and venomous at the same time.

As far as Mrs. Hokum was concerned, the only lessons worth learning were what she called "the positive things in life." Even when she was scolding someone, she always wore a cheerful expression that looked as if it were painted on. "I want to see happy faces in this classroom," she would say, insisting that her students should always have attentive smiles, even though she didn't give them any reason to listen or to be happy. Above her desk she had a poster of the sun rising over a meadow full of daisies, with a quote from a novel, *Candide,* by Voltaire: "All is for the best in the best of all possible worlds!" Mrs. Hokum hadn't actually read *Candide,* otherwise she might not have chosen the poster. The only kinds of books she assigned were those with happy endings, and when she gave a history lesson, she skimmed over all the unpleasant parts, like famines, earthquakes, poverty, plagues, and wars.

In addition to having the most orderly classroom in the school, Mrs. Hokum was always dressed so perfectly that she looked like a mannequin in one of the department stores at the mall, with matching shoes and skirt, and sweaters that never bulged at the elbows or sagged at the wrists. Her perfume had a poisonous sweetness that followed her down the hall. Wherever she walked, the high heels on her shoes clicked like a malevolent metronome. Mrs. Hokum's hair, a reddish blond, was perfectly styled, and whenever the bell rang, she reached for her handbag to redo her lipstick.

On the bulletin board at the back of the classroom was a large display labeled with pink and yellow lettering:

POSITIVE PROFILES OF SELF-ESTEEM

Orion and Ming had agreed that it was one of the dumbest things Mrs. Hokum had done all year. Each of the students in the class had to create a personal profile by answering a list of ten questions designed to highlight his or her best qualities. They also had to include a photograph (smile, please!). Most of the class had tried to impress the teacher with earnest responses, but Orion and Ming couldn't bring themselves to take the profiles seriously. The weekend before the assignment was due they had photographed themselves in a booth at the Cineplex. Orion's face was like a mug shot on a wanted poster. Though he was smiling, it looked as if he had just been to the dentist and got a jaw full of Novocain. He had also turned both eyes to one side. Ming's picture wasn't much better. She had put on a leopard-print beret that she'd bought at a thrift store, and her grin looked as if she were saying "Anchovies!" instead of "Cheese!" Next to both pictures, Mrs. Hokum had written: "Couldn't you find a nicer likeness of yourself?"

The questions were the same for everyone:

1. What do you like best about yourself?
   Ming: My tonsils.
   Orion: My shadow.

2. What did you learn this year that makes you feel proud?

   Ming: Most women have a higher IQ than men.

   Orion: Marshmallow fluff was invented in Massachusetts.

3. If you were a book, what would be your title?

   Ming: *Green Eggs and Ham* by Dr. Seuss.

   Orion: *The Iliad* by Homer Simpson.

4. Give one example of how you have helped someone else.

   Ming: Yesterday I shared my lunch with Orion.

   Orion: Yesterday I helped Ming stick to her diet.

5. What kind of food makes you happy?

   Ming: Anything that isn't healthy.

   Orion: Lowfat ice cubes.

6. What is your greatest achievement?

   Ming: Vacuuming the classroom three times last week.

   Orion: Not laughing when Mr. Abernathy's chair broke during assembly.

7. If you named something after yourself, what would it be?

   Ming: A new flavor of ice cream.

   Orion: A constellation.

8. Which historical figure do you admire most?

   Ming: Genghis Khan's wife.

   Orion: Pac-Man.

9. When you look in the mirror, what makes you smile?
   Ming: My toothbrush.
   Orion: Knowing it's just a reflection.

10. How do you plan to change the world when you grow up?
    Ming: Invent an oblong bowling ball.
    Orion: Become President and paint the White House blue.

Both of them got a C- on their profiles, which didn't have any effect on their self-esteem. Mrs. Hokum had decided who her favorite students were during the first week of class, and after that she picked on everyone else. Someone like Marigold Deitz got an A no matter what she did, while Ming or Orion could get all the answers right on a test and their teacher would still take off points for handwriting or using a pencil instead of a pen. If she didn't like you, there wasn't anything you could do. Even if your parents complained to the principal, Mr. Abernathy would just shake his head and say that Mrs. Hokum was one of the finest, most experienced teachers in the school. The only way to defend yourself was to be as inconspicuous as possible. Fortunately, there were only three more weeks until summer, and after that they would be free of Mrs. Hokum forever.

For the final assignment in social studies the class was being divided into groups. Each had to chose a different country and make a presentation with posters, costumes, and a written report.

"I'm calling it the Carville World's Fair!" said Mrs. Hokum, proudly gesturing with both hands. "We can learn so much from other countries and cultures, don't you think?"

Orion started to roll his eyes, then glanced across at Ming, who was nodding thoughtfully. The look she gave him made it clear she already had a plan in mind. Maybe this wasn't going to be such a boring project after all.

6

palimpsest /ˈpaelimp-sest/ *n.* **1.** writing-material or manuscript on which the original writing has been effaced for reuse. **2.** monumental brass turned and re-engraved on the reverse side. (Greek *palin* again, *psestos* rubbed)

palindrome /ˈpaelin-dreum/ *n.* word or phrase reading the same backwards as forwards (e.g. *nurses run*) **palindromic** /ˈdromik/ *adj.* (Greek *palindromos* running back; related to PALIMPSEST, *drom*-run)

Courtney was so bored she was reading a copy of the *Oxford Dictionary*. Not only had her mother grounded her, but she had unplugged the TV and told Courtney that she couldn't use the computer or speak with her friends on the phone. After coming straight home from school, she finished her homework in half an hour, and now she sat in her room trying to figure out what she could do for the rest of the afternoon. The dictionary offered only limited entertainment. For a while, she even tried to think up palindromes without success.

Agnes, a shaggy golden retriever, lay at the foot of the bed looking guilty. The night before, Courtney had gotten into trouble because Agnes started to bark as she was sneaking back into the house. Courtney's mother had awoken and found her daughter climbing through the window. The dog now wagged her tail apologetically. In frustration, Courtney stood up and went downstairs, where her mother was starting supper.

"Mom, I need to go to the library."

Her mother looked at her with a stern expression of disapproval. "You know you can't go out of the house."

"But I need to get something for school. I've got a report to write. I need to get books." This wasn't completely a lie, but it wasn't entirely the truth.

"Why didn't you tell me this when you came home from school?"

"I forgot," said Courtney. "Please. I've got to go to the library, otherwise I'll get an F."

Agnes had followed her downstairs and now stood in the kitchen, whimpering to be fed.

"I'll be gone for an hour," said Courtney. "Please, Mom. It's important."

"You know you're grounded. I don't want you leaving the house on your own."

"But the library closes at five. I'll go on my bike and I'll be back by suppertime. Promise."

"Well . . . if it's only the library," her mother conceded. "But if you're lying to me and visit your friends, you'll be grounded for the rest of the summer."

Courtney was so relieved she even gave Agnes a pat on the head as she rushed out the door and jumped on her bike, before her mother had a chance to change her mind. Taking a shortcut through the parking lot of the Episcopal church, she got to the library in less than ten minutes.

Locking her bike, she went straight inside and down the steps to the stacks. Ming and Orion were already there, sitting on the floor with *The Compleat Necromancer* open on their knees.

"Hey, what happened? How did you get out?"

"I told my mom I needed to do some research for a report." Courtney grinned. "What have you found?"

"Nothing," said Orion with a glum look. "My flashlight isn't here."

"Any ghosts around?"

"No, but look at this," said Ming. "There's a whole chapter here about a haunted island. Listen to this. . . ."

She began to read from the book:

"The sixth and smallest island of Ilhas dos Fantasmas, known as the Isle of Banished Spirits, is a barren outcropping of rock and sand. This wasteland lies at the eastern end of the archipelago, a stark contrast to the lush green forests of palm trees and tropical foliage that cover the rest of Prithvideep. Even the coral that once surrounded the island has died, a bleached white ring of skeletal reefs, drained of color and bereft of fish.

"None of the islanders dare set foot on this deserted

patch of land, which has a cragged summit strewn with
boulders and caves where even the bats refuse to roost. In
1903, an English freighter[4] was wrecked on the island.
Its crew drowned, but the rusting hulk of the ship can
still be seen, protruding above the reef like the metallic
shell of a giant crustacean, eroding in the waves. Only
the most malicious ghosts—the spirits of vile murderers
and sadistic pirates, tyrant captains and brutal
mutineers—wander these sands. According to legend,
they gather at night on this barren atoll, performing
grotesque rituals and macabre ceremonies that make the
terrible sins they committed in life seem insignificant
compared to the atrocities they practice in death."

Ming had been reading so quickly she had to stop and catch
her breath.

"I don't believe any of this," said Orion, fidgeting uneasily.
"Even if it's written in a book."

"Shshsh!" said Courtney. "Read the rest."

Ming continued:

"If any creature happens to set foot on the island, its fate
is sealed.[5] One year, a flock of migrating terns happened

---

4. The *Elizabethan Dawn* was an 800-ton schooner-rigged tramp steamer, carrying a cargo of soda biscuits and Stilton cheese that kept the fish and lobsters fed for years.

5. If a boat approaches the shore, these desperate and hideous souls gather in a threatening mob, taunting and dancing dangerous jigs on the sand, though they will not enter the water. It is possible, therefore, to approach within twenty or thirty feet without being attacked. The banished spirits also pose for photographs quite readily, making horrible faces at the camera.

to land there by mistake. Within minutes, all that remained of the birds was ash, which blew out to sea like pale gray feathers that disappeared as soon as they touched the waves. On another occasion, a whale beached itself on the Isle of Banished Spirits. Nobody could explain why it would have done such a thing. Most cetaceans know by instinct to avoid the island, but the whale swam through a gap in the reef at high tide and was washed up onto the sand. By the next morning its bones had been picked clean and scattered across the beach, as if the skeleton had been torn apart by a hurricane.

"Worst of all was the tragedy of two fishermen from Prithvideep who went out in a catamaran, casting their nets for mackerel. When a wave capsized their boat, the men swam for the closest land, which happened to be the Isle of Banished Spirits. Too late they realized their mistake and were dragged ashore by the incoming tide. Other fishermen could hear their cries for help, but nobody had the courage to rescue them. As it grew dark, their pleas became more and more desperate. The agonized sound of their torment was unrelenting, wailing and shrieking, pleading for death.[6] Nobody on any of the other islands could sleep that night, for the cries carried on the wind, shrill and painful. Even the families of the fishermen

---

6. The banished spirits often feed their victims to scorpion crabs that nip at their flesh and devour their victims one tiny morsel at a time.

didn't have the courage to go and help them, imagining the cruel tortures inflicted by those evil phantoms. Only at dawn did their anguished voices fall silent. A few weeks later, a raft of bones and seaweed was discovered drifting on the waves. The two men's skulls lay atop the grisly flotsam. When these were carried to shore, the islanders could see marks where the ghosts had gnawed at the joints and sucked marrow from the bones. All of the teeth in the skulls were ground to stubs from gnashing, and the sockets of their eyes were filled with the spines of sea urchins. Not even the sharks inflict such horrors."

Just as Ming finished reading the passage, the three of them heard a cough and looked up to see Alma Parker standing at the end of the row of shelves. She was studying them with a suspicious look on her face, then she held up Orion's flashlight.

"Is this yours?" she asked.

There was a long silence before the three of them nodded.

"What were you doing in the library last night?"

"We were just . . . just exploring," Courtney stammered.

Alma raised a skeptical eyebrow, though she looked more worried than angry.

"Did you find anything . . ." She paused before finishing the question. ". . . Anything unusual?"

"No," all three voices answered at once.

"Show me that book."

Ming handed *The Compleat Necromancer* to the librarian, who opened it and read the title, then glanced up in alarm.

"I don't think you know how much trouble you're in."

"Please don't tell our parents," said Orion.

"That's going to be the least of your worries," said Alma. "Are you sure you didn't see anything last night?"

All three shook their heads, puzzled by the librarian's strange manner.

"Well, I'd like you to leave now," she said sternly. "And I don't want you sneaking around the library at night ever again."

Ming and the others got to their feet and filed past Ms. Parker, who handed Orion his flashlight. On their way out of the stacks, Courtney quickly pulled three books from the shelves at random. Upstairs, she checked them out before leaving the library, then took the books home so her mother wouldn't get suspicious.

7

Memorandum

To: Alma Parker, Head Librarian
Carville Public Library

From: Roberta Hokum, Sixth-Grade Teacher
Carville Middle School

Re: Unacceptable Titles

I want to bring to your attention a number of books in the library that have objectionable titles. A library should be a place where young people are introduced to the positive things in life, rather than depressing, offensive, and disturbing subjects. I strongly suggest that you discard the books listed below and replace them with more wholesome literature.

The Witches by Roald Dahl

Bleak House by Charles Dickens

The Heart of Darkness by Joseph Conrad

As I Lay Dying by William Faulkner

Crime and Punishment by Fyodor Dostoyevsky

A Series of Unfortunate Events by Lemony Snicket

In Cold Blood by Truman Capote

Killer's Kiss by R. L. Stine

Death in the Afternoon by Ernest Hemingway

Nausea by John Paul Sartre

To Kill a Mockingbird by Harper Lee

My Mortal Enemy by Willa Cather

The Murders in the Rue Morgue by Edgar Allan Poe

The Satanic Verses by Salman Rushdie

The Chocolate War by Robert Cormier

There are many more titles like these, and I would be happy to help remove them from the library.

Sincerely,

Roberta Hokum

Alma tossed the memorandum in the wastebasket.

The last thing she needed right now was another complaint from Roberta Hokum. Every month or two, the sixth-grade teacher sent Alma one of these memos, protesting about different things in the library, from the color of the carpets to the magazine subscriptions. It seemed as if Roberta had nothing better to do than poke her nose into the library's business.

Alma cautiously picked up the mysterious book she'd found that morning. Prying it open partway, she saw that the apparition was still there. Quickly closing the book again, she locked it away in her filing cabinet. Alma still didn't know what this image might be, but she was determined to find out. Before she could do anything, however, there were already three other crises at the library that afternoon.

First of all, a three-year-old had gotten loose in the children's section. Unattended by his mother, he had pulled all of the books off the lower shelves, spreading them out on the floor in disarray. Alma asked one of the volunteer librarians to pick up the mess and re-shelve the books. Secondly, two of the computers had frozen up, and no matter how many keys you pressed, nothing appeared on the screen. On top of that, the photocopying machine had a paper jam and refused to accept anything but dimes. Alma hated the photocopier. It was ten years old and kept breaking down at least once a week. As Alma struggled to open the front cover and take out the gnawed and crumpled pieces of paper, she cursed the machine under her breath. Even when it was working, the photocopier made as much noise as a garbage truck and was always demanding more toner or paper. People kept complaining that it took their money and refused to make copies, or printed things the wrong way around. Alma was convinced there was an evil gremlin in the machine.

8

May 26

Something weird is going on. I don't know what
it is but I feel as if we should never have
sneaked into the library last night and
chanted that spell. Reading about the island
of ghosts today gave me the creeps. When I
got home, I started shivering for no reason
and Mom thought I was getting a fever. I
wanted to tell her about what happened but
she'd never understand. I'm really getting
scared. Seriously. It's not like last week when
I went to that movie with O and C—<u>The
Wolverine's Curse</u>. It was rated R but C's mom
let us watch it. Even though it was supposed to
be a horror film, none of us got frightened
and we kept laughing, it was so stupid. But
today I can't stop thinking about that big

green book. Just holding it in my hands made
me feel as if something terrible was going to
happen, as if it was cursed.

Ming had written in her diary every day for the past five years.
Sometimes she scribbled no more than a couple of lines, and on
other days she would fill pages and pages with her thoughts.
Ming kept the diary hidden in a cedar chest at the foot of her
bed, which was full of things she had collected—pinecones from
a trip to New Hampshire last summer, seashells and a petrified
shark's tooth that she found on the beach during a family vacation two years ago in Florida, a T-shirt from the fifth-grade science fair, along with a blue ribbon she'd won for first prize. The
chest was full of objects like these, including a doll she'd been
given years ago by her grandmother. It was missing an arm, but
Ming couldn't bring herself to throw it away. And of course, the
diary—all five volumes, one for every year. Sometimes, before
she wrote a new entry, Ming liked to flip back through the
pages and read some of the earlier passages. Just yesterday she
had written:

May 25
I hate school. Today we had an English test
and we had to identify the different parts of
a poem, the rhyme scheme, the metaphors,
the alliteration, and the meter (which I
got wrong). The poem was written by an
Englishman named John Masefield and I liked
the first stanza:

A wind's in the heart of me, a fire's in my heels,
I am tired of brick and stone and rumbling
wagon wheels,
I hunger for the sea's edge, the limits of the land,
Where the wild old Atlantic is shouting on the sand.

I don't know why I like those lines but it's not
because of the things that we were supposed
to identify for the test. It just sounds like
there's a song in the words and it makes me
want to go sailing, even if I'm afraid of the
ocean and can't swim. This summer I'm going
to take swimming lessons.

May 24

I've decided that I want to become a psychic
when I grow up, telling people about their
future. Today I went to the library and found
a book on palm reading. When I looked at the
lines on my own hand there was something
really strange. My life line is very long, which is
a good thing, but there's a second line that runs
parallel to it and I don't know what that means.
The book doesn't say. I also found another book
called _The Compleat Necromancer_, which is all
about an island full of ghosts. There's even a
spell for summoning spirits. I told C about it
and she wants to try it out. She has this
obsession with supernatural stuff.

May 23

Mrs. H is such a cow. She made us vacuum the classroom carpet during lunch because I was talking with O during math. The whole time Mrs. H just sat there with a fake smile on her face. O says she probably ODs on artificial sweetener every day. He's such a dork but he's the only person that can make me laugh.

Between the pages of her diary, Ming had tucked away some of the things she had collected. There were a couple of maple leaves picked last fall. When she first pressed them inside the diary, they had been a fiery red and gold color, but now they were a dull brown. One of the leaves had crumbled, and she brushed away the dry fragments to see the outline of the leaf still printed on the page, superimposed over her handwriting. At another place in her diary, she had a photograph of Courtney, Orion, and herself, standing in front of a doughnut shop. Ming liked the picture because they all looked as if they were holding their breath. Farther back in the diary, almost a year ago, she had clipped out an article from the *Carville Gazette*. It was about a decomposed body discovered in a cranberry bog on the edge of town. In the margin of the clipping Ming had jotted, "No more cranberry juice for me."

While Ming was writing in her journal, Orion was in his room playing a new video game—*Kiernan's Castle.* The first few levels were easy, but once he got through the enchanted forest and across the drawbridge, things started to get complicated. Instead of the leprechauns and four-leaf clovers that kept popping up in his path, now there were screaming banshees and glowing daggers. The whole castle was a maze, full of trapdoors, dead-end passageways, and spiral staircases. Orion had to turn the volume down so his parents wouldn't hear. They thought he was doing his homework, but he had already finished. The only annoying thing about the game were the sound effects, cheesy Celtic music full of whistles and jingles. So far, he had fought off three banshees and two ghouls that came at him with green cudgels. Orion held the controller tightly in both hands, his thumbs moving deftly over the buttons. As he stabbed one of the banshees with a dagger, he thought about the Isle of Banished Spirits. He didn't like the sound of that place and preferred his ghosts and ghouls in digital form, where he could fend them off with a flick of his thumb. Now he was climbing one of the towers of Kiernan's Castle, and skeletons were hanging in chains from the walls. Suddenly, a swarm of bats came swooping down the stairs and sent him tumbling into the moat. Immediately, a swamp serpent caught him by the neck and started strangling him in its coils. Orion kept pressing the right-hand key on the controller, though the glowing dagger had disappeared. He tried to flip around and throw the serpent off, but nothing seemed to work. The coils drew tighter and tighter, like a suffocating knot. There was no escape. Gradually the screen went dark and a message appeared:

Y're Dead!

Fortunately, he had another life.

9

Nick sat in front of the window overlooking the garden, separated from the world outside by thick panes of clear glass. Like fish inside an aquarium, his eyes drifted back and forth, observing the morning sunlight pouring through a flowering dogwood tree. He sat alone with his thoughts, unable to step outside and feel the fresh-cut grass tickle the soles of his bare feet or smell the lilac bushes in bloom. Spring. Almost summer. Seasons passed by the window as if in another world, removed from the still, suffocating air inside. Within these walls it was always warm and dry. Each breath Nick took was tinged with a chemical sweetness. Outside there were new leaves and pollen, green ferns unrolling their feathery heads, bees and mayflies. Inside there were plastic flowers that remained bright and odorless all year. Instead of the whirring of insect wings there was only the soft murmur of electric fans.

In his mind, Nick saw the ocean of his youth, low tide crashing over a coral lip, rumpled clouds along the horizon like a farther reef, as if the sky itself were breaking in waves. He could see the fishermen in their bobbing catamarans.

I know this place.

I am at home in the water.

I swim with the dolphins that sculpt the waves, leaping through the salt spray.

I put my head below the surface and watch the flicking blue of tiny darters, the languid swarms of surgeonfish, the colors of coral glinting in the wavering sunlight.

I hear the sad songs of whales.

A grandfather clock chimed at the far end of the room, the sound dissolving his thoughts. He turned to look over his shoulder. The pale, papery features of his face were almost translucent, the white eyebrows and thin hair, the tattoo on his cheek, like a faded bruise.

A nurse came through the door and greeted him. She was young with yellow hair.

"Hi, Nick! Beautiful day, isn't it? Makes you want to go to the beach."

The old man didn't answer as she wheeled him away from the window.

"What about that storm last night! Wasn't that something, all that thunder and lightning? Did you hear it?"

The nurse spoke to him as if he were a child, though the old man was three times her age. When he replied, his voice was hoarse and the words came from another language, a foreign tongue. Not understanding him, the nurse went on speaking about the weather and telling him how she planned to go shopping over the weekend.

She wheeled him down the corridor, past a dozen doors and into his room, the one marked NICODEMUS OSGOOD. Another window looked out onto the street, where cars shuttled past the gate of the Hornswoggle Bay Nursing Home.

Adjusting the collar on the old man's pajamas, the nurse patted his shoulder.

"Now don't get into any trouble, Nick," she said.

He looked away from her, toward a shelf beside his bed. After the nurse had left, the old man slowly wheeled himself across the room. Stretching out his arm, he could just reach an instrument on the shelf. It looked like a wooden bowl. Taking it down, he held it in both hands.

The instrument was a thumb piano, made from half a coconut shell. It was simply constructed with an arched bridge across the center, carved out of whale bone. Attached to this were a dozen metal tines, flattened at the ends. The coconut shell had been etched with floral patterns, and its hollow cup gave resonance to the notes.

Stooped in his wheelchair, the old man cradled the thumb piano in his hands, staring down at it, as if in a trance. His thin, bony fingers held the bowl of the coconut shell, and his thumbs were positioned on the keys. For several minutes there was silence before he pressed one of the tines, sending out a plaintive note. At first he seemed to pick at the keys without any rhythm, but gradually the music took shape—a slow, syncopated beat like the first drops of rain on a tin roof. The notes were clearer now, as the old man's fingers moved up and down the scale. Vibrations filled the sterile room with a haunting melody.

10

The books that Courtney had checked out sat on her desk unopened. She had finished supper and had been sent to her room, not allowed to watch TV. Though Courtney was relieved her trip to the library hadn't ended in disaster, she was puzzled by Ms. Parker's behavior. The librarian seemed to know more than she was letting on.

Lying on her bed with Agnes, Courtney stroked the dog's silky ears and tried to imagine what a ghost would actually look like. She didn't really believe in them, at least not the kind that walked through walls or rattled their bones. In movies ghosts were always unconvincing, hovering about like a cloud of fireflies or disappearing into closets like fog blowing through a window. Even though she was skeptical about spirits and spooks, Courtney couldn't help but wonder if they might exist, somewhere in the margins of the world around her. She thought of them as penciled images that had been erased, leaving only the faintest impression.

On the way to school and back each day, Courtney rode her

bicycle past the town cemetery, and she often wondered if it was haunted. The graveyard looked so orderly and peaceful, she couldn't imagine the spirits of dead people drifting up out of the ground. Headstones stood in neat rows with clusters of flags and flowers arranged in front of them. Ancient oaks and maples overshadowed the cemetery, but there was nothing spooky about those trees and the shade they cast. The graveyard was a quiet, unthreatening park, even if there were hundreds of decaying bodies buried six feet underground.

Last year, for Halloween, Courtney had dressed up as a ghost, but instead of wearing a sheet with holes for eyes, she had painted her face a neon blue and teased her hair into a wild mane, braided with strands of silver tinsel. She blackened her eyes so they looked like hollow sockets. Using her mother's brightest lipstick, she gave herself a bloodred mouth and put her clothes on backwards so it looked as if her body were facing the wrong direction. Instead of shoes she wore her Rollerblades, swooping down the sidewalk in the dark, like a restless spirit traveling on the wind. Even Ming and Orion had trouble seeing through her disguise.

But all of that had been a game, a costume that she put on. Courtney knew she was getting too old for Halloween, and the whole thing had been a joke, meant to frighten the younger neighborhood kids who were trick-or-treating on the street. What she really wanted to do was scare herself.

On the walls of her room she had posters of weird images—a black-and-white print of an Egyptian mummy with scarab beetles crawling out of its eyes, a copy of an oil painting by the Dutch artist Hieronymous Bosch depicting tormented spirits condemned to hell, a photograph of a raven perched on a dead branch. She also had a plastic devil mask that she'd found at a yard sale. It had bulging eyes, chiseled fangs, and a necklace of skulls around its neck. On her dressing table was a mirror that Courtney had draped with a black lace veil that looked like cobwebs. She had also put glow-in-the-dark stickers of cats' eyes on the mirror, so that when she turned the lights off at night, these shone with an eerie green aura. Her mother kept complaining that the room was depressing, but Courtney liked it the way it was.

Getting up from her bed now, she went across to her wardrobe and took out a pair of candles, which had burned down halfway so the metal stands were coated with melted wax. Putting these on her desk and lighting them, Courtney switched off the bedside lamp. Her room was bathed in a flickering glow and the candles gave off a smoky fragrance. With the shades drawn, everything seemed closer and more intimate. The only sound was Agnes whimpering softly in her dreams as she chased imaginary squirrels.

Still bored and not at all sleepy, Courtney switched on her bedside lamp again and reached for one of the books—*Economic Trends in the Twentieth Century*. It was a thin paperback with a wrinkled cover, and when she opened it two of the pages came loose. There were a few charts and diagrams, but nothing interesting. Setting it aside, she picked up the second book—*A Statistical Analysis of the Maritime Trade*. This one looked even more boring, but when Courtney opened the cover she saw the bookplate with the design of palm trees and the inkstand and quill pen. She also noticed the name *Hezekiah T. Osgood* written on the fly leaf in faded blue ink. The signature looked like a tangled thread. At that moment, the pages began to riffle in her hands.

As the book opened on its own, Courtney almost dropped it to the floor. She blinked her eyes a couple of times, unwilling to believe what she was seeing. There was something slippery between the pages, like onionskin paper, a translucent layer that blurred the words. Placing the book on her bed, Courtney saw a faint image—a yellowish sepia color. It was almost invisible, like the pale outline of a fern that might have been pressed inside the book long ago. But the image was moving slowly, flowing together into a woman's face. Her features were delicate and her skin was dark. As the woman's eyes came into focus, Courtney sucked in her breath. It was like looking into a mirror, except the reflection was someone else's. The woman's black hair was pulled to one side and fell across her shoulder. She wore a collarless blouse, and around her neck was a string of coral beads.

The apparition seemed to be singing, though at first there wasn't any sound, only the movement of her lips. For several minutes, Courtney sat frozen on the bed as the woman's voice grew audible, the muted song drifting into the room. Though she could feel every nerve in her body trembling, Courtney tried to stay calm, telling herself that she had to be dreaming. But now the woman turned to look at her, watching the girl with a quizzical expression.

"Who are you?" Courtney whispered.

It seemed to take several seconds before her words reached the woman's ears.

The singer stopped abruptly and squinted her eyes as if she were peering through a curtain of shadows. Then she shook her head and spoke, except the words made no sense. Courtney couldn't understand what the woman was saying, though she knew it was some kind of question.

Before she could reply, Agnes started to growl. The dog was on her feet, hackles raised. The woman inside the book seemed frightened and began to shrink back into the page.

"Wait, don't go!" said Courtney, then to the dog, who had let out a loud bark of alarm, she said, "Stop it, Agnes! No!"

A moment later she heard her mother's footsteps coming down the hall. In a panic, Courtney closed the book, and the strange woman disappeared.

"Are you all right?" her mother asked, putting her head inside the door. "Why did Agnes bark?"

"It's nothing," said Courtney, out of breath. "I think it's just raccoons outside, that's all."

After her mother left, she took another quick look to make sure the woman was still there. Opening the book a couple of inches, Courtney could just make out the ghostly profile on the page.

11

Her name is Nalini. She is the youngest daughter of Philome-nia and Prithvi Sangarajan. In 1729 she dies of an equatorial fever, one of many victims of an epidemic that kills off half the population of the islands in a single year. The first appearance of the ghosts on Ilhas dos Fantasmas coincides with this epidemic.

Nalini is eighteen when she dies. Until then she lives a happy, carefree life. As a young child she often sings when she speaks, giving the simplest words or phrases a musical note. Her brothers and sisters tease her, calling her a songbird, like one of the curlews that migrate all the way from Siberia to Ilhas dos Fantasmas during the winter months. Even on those rare occasions when Nalini is sad, her words take on a lyrical tone of melancholy. As she grows older, she learns many of the folk songs of the islands—some are old sea shanties, others are nursery rhymes and lullabies, and some are nostalgic ballads that recall homes left behind. In the evenings, around a fire of burning coconut husks, Nalini often sings these songs to entertain her family and friends, her voice clear and fluid as the curlew's call.

There is no school on the islands when Nalini is growing up, and whatever she learns comes from her parents, as well as her own experiences. She has the kind of curiosity that always takes her one step further than the rest of her friends, overturning every rock in her path to find crabs and sand lions hiding underneath, or swimming out beyond the reef to chase the dolphins that circle the island at low tide. Sometimes her impulsive sense of exploration gets her into trouble, like the time she climbs to the top of a coconut tree to see a palm squirrel's nest. Once she reaches the crown of leaves, she can't climb down again and has to be rescued by her father.

Almost everything catches Nalini's interest, and she entertains herself by counting the different kinds of shells on the beach, or collecting the cocoons of scallop moths. Nalini keeps all kinds of pets, tropical fish in old bottles, pineapple beetles, even a green moss snake, which isn't poisonous. Most of these pets are set free before they realize that they have been captured. The only creature that stays with Nalini for more than a few days is a gecko that she has tamed. It is about six inches long, a dark cinnamon color. The gecko has tiny suction cups on the ends of its toes and perches on her shoulder, or in the hollow of her collar bone, or just behind her ear. It is perfectly camouflaged against her skin, and most people don't notice the gecko until it moves its tail or flicks its tongue. The gecko makes a soft chirping sound, a bit like a chuckle, as if it is laughing as well. Though she doesn't give the gecko a name, Nalini feels as if it has become a part of herself, climbing up her arm or around the collar of her blouse, its delicate fingers pressed against her throat.

After a year and a half, the gecko disappears. Nalini isn't sure if it has wandered off or if it is dead, but her tiny friend is gone forever. She searches for it in the rafters of her house and in the garden, but there is no sign of the gecko. Sometimes, however, she hears a chuckling sound behind her ear and feels the tickling movement of its feet against her skin. For a moment, she thinks that the gecko has crept back onto her shoulder, but when she raises her hand to touch it, nothing is there. Years later, these phantom sensations continue, even after Nalini dies, as if the gecko has followed her into the afterlife.

Trapped inside the book, her tenses blur together—what was, what is, what might come to be—all are the same. Even those brief moments when the pages open, and Nalini looks out at the girl staring down at her, seem part of a constant thread of images that have no beginning or end. The girl is asking questions. Nalini tries to reply, but her voice is garbled, as if her words have passed through a mirror of sound.

Now that the girl has vanished and Nalini is pressed between the pages once again, she is aware of the absence of those she's lost. In the papery shadows that enclose her, she can feel the gecko crawling across the surface of the page, just as it moved over her skin, the gentle suction of its toes clinging to her in the darkness.

12

The natives of Ilhas dos Fantasmas take for granted the presence of ghosts, which they call arora. *They are not frightened of these spirits, except for the evil phantoms restricted to the Isle of Banished Spirits. Elsewhere, the living inhabitants mingle quite happily with the dead. According to the latest census, fifty-three arora have been counted on Ilhas dos Fantasmas, along with a sentient population of 234. . . .*

No ghosts were hiding between the pages of *The Compleat Necromancer*, but Hezekiah Osgood's words gave Alma Parker an uneasy feeling. Closing the library at five o'clock, she took the heavy green volume home with her. Once dinner was over and her husband, Ted, was safely watching a Red Sox baseball game on TV, the librarian settled into a comfortable wing-backed chair in the living room and picked up the book again. Though Alma had considered telling Ted about her strange experience that morning, she decided to keep it to herself until she had a clearer idea of what was going on. Ted Parker taught chemistry at Carville High School, and Alma knew he would think she was crazy if she told him she'd seen a ghost.

Ordinarily, Alma preferred reading novels, poetry, or biographies, and sometimes murder mysteries. If she had picked up this book yesterday, it wouldn't have interested her at all. The idea of spirits inhabiting an island somewhere in the Indian Ocean would have seemed so ridiculous to her that she wouldn't have given the book a second glance. But having come face-to-face with a ghost that morning, the gauzy apparition still haunted her. She wanted an explanation, even if she didn't completely believe what she had seen.

Though Alma had flipped through *The Compleat Necromancer* briefly, after taking it away from Ming, this time she began reading from the beginning of the book. Hezekiah Osgood described his first encounter with an arora, which took place only a few hours after he'd set foot on the island. Having gone to collect drinking water from a spring, the professor was filling a jug when he noticed "a slight movement in the underbrush, as if a bird was darting about in the leaves." Moments later, he looked up to see a woman standing in front of him. Hezekiah was startled that she had approached so silently. Her appearance was unusual, the translucent complexion of her skin and her pale gray eyes, but this was nothing compared to what he witnessed next. Without a sound, the woman turned aside and disappeared, as if she had passed through an invisible door. One moment she was facing him, and the next instant the woman was gone. It was like "an atmospheric mirage that leaves no shadow in its wake."

After recounting how this strange woman appeared and disappeared a dozen times within an hour, Professor Osgood went on to explain the nature of these arora, beginning with their physical characteristics:

> *They have neither mass nor volume, no third dimension by which we might measure their presence. But to say these ghosts are flat, as if printed on a sheet of paper, would be inaccurate. Looking at them head-on, their features appear to have depth and seem quite lifelike. As soon as they turn away, however, the image evaporates. It is impossible to describe exactly what they are made of, for none of the rules of physics or biology apply. They cannot be classified according to the established laws of science.[7]*

At this point, the professor digressed into a lengthy discussion about how these arora represented "an optical and temporal phenomenon." He speculated whether they shared some of the same properties as starlight since the spirits seemed to emit a sidereal glow, as if they were composed of ancient light.

Alma skimmed most of this section, moving ahead to the next chapter in which Osgood went on to explain that while it was impossible to touch a ghost, they were capable of touching the living— "a paradox that defies logic but is invariably true." For example, if

---

7. Osgood goes on to compare the images to reflections in a mirror or handheld looking glass, in which the image disappears when the mirror is turned at an angle. He also uses the term "spectral refractions."

he put out a hand to grab the arm of a ghost, it was like reaching into an empty closet, but at the same time these spirits were perfectly able to catch hold of a human being. A person could be pulled or patted, bitten, pinched, or even caressed by an arora, but there could be no physical response in return.

One of the many unusual characteristics of these phantoms, Osgood recorded, was that they avoided water and were unable to travel from one island to the next. Though they seemed to drift just above the land, even on the calmest day, they were never seen upon the ocean and refused to set foot in a boat. Similarly, whenever there was rain, the phantoms took shelter inside dry crevices of rocks or empty seashells.

> *The effects of water on the arora are not severe but cause mildly unpleasant symptoms, intermittent sneezing and a spectral rash that blurs their image for a day or two, somewhat like a lens that has fogged up with moisture.*[8]

Fire, on the other hand, seemed to have fatal consequences for the spirits. If a ghost came in contact with any kind of flame, even a burning candle, the spirit was consumed immediately and nothing survived. For the arora, fire meant a second and final death.[9]

Being a scholar from the Learned Society for the Elucidation of Primitive Cultures, Osgood also investigated the social,

---

8. Osgood also points out that according to barometric readings he took on Ilhas dos Fantasmas, the ghosts are most likely to appear when humidity in the atmosphere is low and they vanish as soon as the barometer begins to drop.

9. As an example, Osgood cites the case of an arora that wandered too close to a bonfire and came in contact with a flying cinder. Instantly, the ghost dissolved into flames.

psychological, and ethical characteristics of the arora. He claimed to know as much about these spirits as he did about the human inhabitants of Prithvideep. From his observations:

> The society of ghosts is not very different from ours, though they tend to live more solitary lives and exhibit few strong sentiments or emotions. It is difficult to know what they are feeling. Sometimes they appear contented and at other moments melancholia shrouds their features, but all of this is expressed with enigmatic subtlety.

As Alma continued to read, she felt a combination of curiosity and disbelief. The whole thing seemed made up, like some sort of fairy tale, though she kept reminding herself that earlier that day she had actually seen a ghost. (That book remained locked away in her filing cabinet, where it would stay until she got up the nerve to open it again.) Alma couldn't deny that the boy's image, pressed between those pages, seemed to match the description of an arora.

The chapter on "The Purpose and Practice of Necromancy" left her feeling even more unsettled. Alma had never had any interest in psychics and séances, dismissing them as nonsense. In her mind, communicating with the dead was nothing but a hoax that was used to prey on superstitious people. But despite her doubts, she felt a strange uneasiness as Osgood described how the necromancers on Prithvideep were able to talk with the spirits as if they were neighbors chatting across a fence.

She was surprised to learn that the ghosts of Prithvideep were actually able to speak, "though their language is a separate dialect from what is spoken by the islanders." According to Osgood, only a few people on Prithvideep were able to communicate with the arora in this language. He himself had learned enough to speak to them in a limited manner, though he observed some children were able to speak to the arora with total fluency.

Alma was puzzled by some of the vocabulary the professor used, but she was able to consult a glossary at the end of the book, which contained a list of words with ghostly equivalents. The most interesting part, she found, was Osgood's discussion of the musical traits of the spirit world. It seemed that ghosts were drawn to certain tonal patterns and melodies. Not every kind of music appealed to them, and Osgood had tested different variations. In 1929, he purchased an old wind-up gramophone from a ship that dropped anchor at Prithvideep. He set up the record player in an isolated grove of gum trees, which he knew was a gathering spot for ghosts. The gramophone, its large brass horn opening like a gilded lily, had come with an assortment of twenty-three records, most of which were classical recordings from the Philadelphia Philharmonic Orchestra. Through a series of experiments, Hezekiah discovered that the arora were drawn to Brahms or Beethoven, and Mozart to a lesser degree, but Puccini's arias sent them flying to the farthest corners of the island. There was also a recording of Gilbert and Sullivan's *Mikado* that seemed to have the same effect. The two most popular records, however, were ragtime jazz by a pianist named Gnimble Pickins, whose musical improvisations always attracted an appreciative audience.[10] The arora insisted that

---

10. Gnimble Pickens is best known for his composition "Bleu Cheese Blues," first recorded in 1923.

Osgood play these tunes again and again, until his arms ached from winding up the gramophone and the needle began to skip.

The professor concluded that the syncopated rhythms of the jazz pianist were the sweetest music to a spirit's ear. This was confirmed by his discussions with two necromancers on the islands, both of them over a hundred years old.[11] Their names were Helena and Corpus D'Souza, and they lived together in a small hut made of palm fronds, on an isthmus connecting two halves of the largest island. This couple had no children and they devoted their lives to communicating with spirits. Both understood the language of ghosts with complete fluency and even spoke it between themselves. Much of their day was spent erecting wind harps made with shells and bits of metal or glass that they strung from the branches of trees. Whenever a breeze set the harps in motion they played a natural symphony of notes. These instruments attracted the spirits as surely as the gramophone. According to Helena and Corpus D'Souza, their wind harps had healing properties and cured the ghosts of various ailments and afflictions. It soothed ethereal fevers from which many of the arora suffered. The chiming of the wind harps eased the pain of spectral boils and blisters or provided relief from a chronic kind of ghostly arthritis. There was even a specific harp constructed to drive away phantasmal lice, an annoying parasite that infested many of the ghosts.[12]

For three and a half hours that evening, Alma pored over the book, trying to understand what was haunting her library.

---

11. Osgood notes that there were at least six other necromancers on the island.
12. There are also unconfirmed reports of a spectral leech that attaches itself to phantoms and drains their light.

(Fortunately, Ted's baseball game went into extra innings.) Though she was intrigued by Hezekiah Osgood's observations on Ilhas dos Fantasmas, she couldn't help but distrust him. There was something sinister about the scholarly tone of his writing and the cold, clinical way in which he discussed the arora, as if they were specimens that he was planning to dissect.

Osgood's final chapter on "Optical Experiments and Occult Photography" explained his efforts to capture images of the arora. One of the many things he had brought with him to Prithvideep was a camera—a bulky apparatus that stood on a heavy tripod, with a black hood that covered the photographer. Each of the plates had to be prepared ahead of time, painted with a syrupy emulsion and dipped in a solution of silver nitrate that reacted to light. Osgood's first experiments ended in failure. Though he was able to focus the camera on several ghosts and take their photographs, when these were developed, nothing was there—an empty scene without any figures.

At this point, he began to test different chemical combinations and found that if he used a powerful magnesium flash, a faint outline—hardly recognizable—appeared on the negative. He also discovered that the resin from a certain species of gum tree (*Glutinous luminosa*) that grew on the island had photosensitive properties.[13] Meanwhile, he had realized that the images of the arora were very similar to old-fashioned daguerreotype pictures. He immediately sent a telegram to Paris, ordering one of these cameras,

---

13. Osgood explains that the bark of these remarkable trees is used by some of the islanders to create star charts because it captures the light from distant galaxies and constellations.

which in 1930 were already obsolete. Osgood repeated his experiments without success, though a tantalizing blur appeared on several of the polished daguerreotype plates.

It was only after another two years that he finally made his breakthrough. Observing that the images of the ghosts were similar to stereoscope photographs, he inserted a double lens to create this effect. Meanwhile, Osgood also consulted one of the necromancers on Prithvideep, an Australian named Ivan Scuttlebutt. With Scuttlebutt's help, Osgood was able to successfully lure the arora in front of his camera and make them hold still long enough to be photographed. By now he had also dismantled the two cameras and constructed a completely new device that combined the components of both.

Alma skipped over the technical details and diagrams about the camera. The thought that all of Osgood's research had ended up in her library was unnerving. At points while reading, she felt like throwing the book aside in disgust, and other times she was afraid to turn the page.

The professor explained that Scuttlebutt's favorite method of attracting ghosts was to use a crude musical instrument made from the lower half of a human skull. One day as the necromancer played his tunes, Osgood adjusted his camera and ducked beneath the black shroud. Moments later, one of the arora arrived. As soon as the spirit appeared in the viewfinder, Professor Osgood pressed the camera's trigger. A blinding flash erupted with a cloud of smoke that smelled like fireworks.

The ghost instantly disappeared. When Osgood developed the photograph, he found that he had captured not just a likeness of the arora, but the phantom itself. There on the glass plate was the image, reduced in size but complete in every other way. And the most remarkable thing of all was that the ghost in the photograph actually moved. The arora gestured and spoke, but its image remained transfixed on the glass plate.

13

Standing at the front of her classroom, Mrs. Hokum scratched a pink fingernail across the blackboard, where she had drawn a large smiley face.

"Remember, I want cheerful students today!" she said as her lipstick crinkled at the corners of her upturned mouth. "No frowns. No scowls. No sullen faces!"

The only thing that made Orion happy was that there were just twelve more school days. He was looking forward to the summer vacation, when he could sleep until noon and not have to think about homework until September.

"I want you to begin your final projects today," the teacher continued. "Get into your groups, and if you haven't done it already, choose a country that you'll report on for the Carville World's Fair."

There was a moment of hesitation before everyone started to shift their seats and form themselves into groups. Orion and Ming were teamed up with Marigold Deitz.

"I think we should do our report on Canada," said Marigold. "Last winter I went to Montreal."

"That's boring," said Orion. "Canada isn't very different from America."

"They speak French," said Marigold. *"Parlez-vous?"*

"No," said Ming. "We need some other country."

"Okay," said Marigold. "What about Hawaii?"

The other two looked at her and shook their heads.

"I was thinking Ilhas dos Fantasmas," said Ming.

Orion was startled. Just thinking about the Isle of Banished Spirits made him squirm.

"What?" said Marigold. "Where?"

As Ming started to explain, she smelled a sickly sweet perfume, and Mrs. Hokum appeared behind Orion's shoulder. He jumped in his seat when the teacher spoke.

"Well?" she asked. "What have you decided?"

Before Marigold could say anything, Ming spoke up, "We've chosen the smallest country in the world. It's called Ilhas dos Fantasmas."

Their teacher's smile looked like a scowl turned upside down. She shook her head.

"I've never heard of it. Are you sure it's a country?"

"Yes," said Orion, glancing at Ming uncertainly. "It's near the equator in the Indian Ocean. Sometimes it's also called Prithvideep."

Mrs. Hokum's penciled eyebrows went up an inch, and she pursed her lips in disapproval.

"Why don't you choose something in Europe?"

"I suggested Hawaii," said Marigold.

"If we find it in the atlas, Mrs. Hokum, will you let us do our report on Ilhas dos Fantasmas?" asked Ming.

For a moment it looked as if their teacher were going to refuse, but then she nodded reluctantly. Before Mrs. Hokum could change her mind, Orion got up and brought the world atlas from the shelf. It was as big as his desk, and finding the Indian Ocean took a while because it was divided into separate sections on different pages. First they located a map of India, then another that depicted the east coast of Africa and the island of Madagascar, but there was no sign of Prithvideep. They also found a map of Antarctica, but the ocean was cut off below the Tropic of Capricorn. On every page it seemed as if the islands lay just beyond the margins. When they turned to the Arabian peninsula, the Indian Ocean filled the lower half of the map but still not far enough to reach Ilhas dos Fantasmas. They found other islands—Zanzibar, The Seychelles, The Maldives, Mauritius and Diego Garcia—but not what they were looking for. Flipping back and forth through the atlas, Ming and Orion tried to match the lines of longitude and latitude while Marigold watched with an annoyed expression.

"I don't think you know what you're talking about," she said. "I wish we could just do Canada. That would be so much easier. *Très bien.*"

"It has to be here," said Orion as Ming turned to a map of Sri Lanka, which included a large section of the Indian Ocean.

"There it is!" said Ming, pointing to a tiny cluster of dots in the lower left-hand corner of the map. They were barely visible, and the name was printed so faintly it looked like a smudge.

Marigold squinted at the map as if she didn't believe the islands were actually there. Orion and Ming carried the atlas over to Mrs. Hokum's desk. With a skeptical expression, their teacher took out her glasses and peered down at the specks on the page.

"Are you sure it's an independent country?"

"Yes, it used to belong to Portugal. Now it's a republic," said Orion, remembering some of the history Ming had read to him and Courtney.

"All right," said Mrs. Hokum, grudgingly. "But if you can't find enough information, you'll have to choose another country."

After the lunch bell rang, Courtney was waiting for Ming and Orion near the lockers. She had her backpack slung over one shoulder and beckoned for them to follow her.

"What's up?" Ming asked.

"Something serious," she said, leading them into a stairwell that went up to the roof of the school. The door at the top was locked, but there was a landing where nobody would disturb them. Unzipping her backpack, Courtney took out *A Statistical Analysis of the Maritime Trade*.

"That definitely looks serious," said Orion.

Courtney ignored him and opened the book slowly, as if it were a trapdoor. Ming and Orion glanced at each other, wondering if their friend had lost her mind. At the same moment, though, they saw the apparition.

"Omigod!"

"Whoa!"

In the dim light of the stairwell, the woman's eyes looked back at them with glistening intensity. There was an unmistakable sadness about her face, a lost expression, as if she were trapped.

"You see, it worked!" said Courtney.

"What worked?" said Orion, who had stepped back against the wall, as far as he could go.

"The spell," said Courtney. "The incantation we recited in the library. It summoned this ghost."

"What's she doing inside a book?" said Ming.

"I don't know, but she can talk. Except I can't figure out what language she's speaking."

As soon as Courtney said this, all three of them could hear the woman's voice. At first it was like a hushed echo, but gradually it became more distinct. One of her hands was gesturing.

"Maybe she wants us to touch her," said Courtney.

"No way!" Orion edged closer to the stairs.

"Come on, she doesn't look like she'll hurt us," said Courtney.

"I think she wants us to get her out of the book. Maybe if one of us gives her a hand," said Ming.

"You do it," Orion said, his voice cracking.

The image of the ghost remained flat with the page, though it seemed as if it were stuck to the paper like some kind of lamination. Courtney felt an urge to pick at a corner and try to peel it off.

"Okay," she said. "I'll do it, but you've got to hold the book."

Ming nodded. Her hands were sweating.

"I wouldn't do that if I were you," said Orion. His legs and knees were shaking so much they felt as if they might run away on their own.

"Why not? We've got to help her if we can," Courtney insisted.

She stretched out her right hand, but just to make sure, she held on to the railing. Her eyes were fixed on the woman, alert to any sign of danger. As her hand got closer to the image, she expected to feel something, either warm or cold, but there was nothing, no sensation at all. Her fingers brushed the page. It was as if no ghost were there, just the smooth surface of the paper beneath a patina of light.

"There isn't anything here," said Courtney.

"Look!" Ming whispered. "It's like she's trying to reach out and touch you."

There seemed to be an invisible barrier between them, not like a wall or even a pane of glass, but something that separated one dimension from the other.

"What if you turn the page?" said Ming. "Maybe that will bring her closer."

Courtney lifted the corner of the page and flipped it over. Instantly, the ghost was gone, and all they could see were dense paragraphs of print. The next few pages were exactly the same, nothing but words and numbers. Ming turned to the front of the book. On the inside cover was the bookplate with the three palm trees, the inkstand and quill, and a conch shell with wings.

"Isn't that the same symbol from the other book?"

"And Hezekiah T. Osgood. He's the author of *The Compleat Necromancer*. This book used to belong to him."

"That must be it," said Courtney. "He must have brought the ghost with him from Ilhas dos Fantasmas."

"But—but that was a long time ago. Why hasn't anybody else discovered it yet?" Orion tried to control his stammer.

"Who would ever want to read *A Statistical Analysis of the Maritime Trade*?" said Ming. "I bet it's never been checked out."

"No, that's not the point," said Courtney. "The incantation. When we said those words together it must have made the ghost visible."

"Let's see if she's still there," said Ming.

She let the book fall open in her hands, and the ghost reappeared, staring up at them from the page. At first, Orion had thought the image looked a bit like a television screen, but it wasn't like that at all. Instead, the face was really there, not something broadcast from a satellite or transmitted by cable or antennae. Orion could tell that the woman was right in front of them, except that her image was pressed onto the page.

"She looks like she's going to cry," said Ming, carefully putting out her hand to try and touch the ghost. When she ran her fingers over the page, it didn't disturb the image. The woman raised her own hand, staring up at them with anguished eyes.

"Look at her cheek," said Courtney. "It's a tattoo. The same symbol of the seashell with wings."

14

Nalini peers up at the three faces looking down at her and recognizes the girl who first opened the book, the one with dusty brown hair and defiant eyes. The other two children look scared. Nalini hasn't seen or spoken to anyone in years, though she can't remember exactly how long it has been. Instinctively, she calls out a name:

"D'Kele! D'Kele are you there?"

The children look puzzled. There is no reply.

D'Kele is the young man Nalini would have married if she hadn't died a month before their wedding day, one of the first victims of the epidemic. She still remembers the emotions in D'Kele's eyes and the touch of his hands on her face, the muted sound of his voice.

D'Kele is a star-catcher, and he shows Nalini how he makes the sacred bark cloth to capture the light of the stars. Together the two of them spread the scrolls on the beach at night, and D'Kele recites the ancient incantations. They sit together for hours as the night sky wheels above them; they whisper in each other's ears and wait for the patterns to form on the cloth. D'Kele knows when the constellations have turned far enough to leave their mark, and he offers a prayer to the heavens, then gathers the scrolls and takes them home with him. The next day, he reads the future in the curved patterns that appear on the cloth, tracing the movement of the stars like an alphabet of light. From these markings he can foretell the future, the hopes and desires of his people, and the tragedies that will befall them. D'Kele has seen that the epidemic is coming, and he knows that Nalini will be a victim of the fever. But he is forbidden to reveal these things as part of an oath every star-catcher takes.

When Nalini dies, D'Kele performs her final rites, laying her body on a bier of palm fronds that is floated out to sea. Wave burials are a tradition on the islands, a sacred ritual of death. Rather than internment or cremation, the people of Prithvideep consign their corpses to the sea, letting the Bromeil current carry their remains beyond the horizon. Refusing to leave his lover's side, D'Kele swims next to Nalini's funeral raft. The ocean is quiet, and as the shoreline recedes, D'Kele is comforted by the gentle swells. He can see dolphin fish accompanying them beneath the surface, their iridescent colors reflecting the sunlight in brilliant hues. Nalini's face looks calm, her body no longer shaken by the terrible fever but rocking peacefully on the waves. D'Kele is a strong swimmer, though he surrenders himself to the sea, letting the current pull them away from the islands, into the infinite blue waters.

For most of the day, the two lovers drift side by side. When the sun starts to go down, Nalini's bier begins to sink, and she gradually descends beneath the surface. D'Kele knows that he will drown with her but does not care, imagining the two of them falling slowly into the ocean, through clouds of mackerel and swarms of angelfish.

As Nalini's body begins to slide away beneath him, D'Kele dives down to touch her one last time. The palm fronds can no longer bear her weight but slow her sinking form, as if she were riding a kite. The star-catcher holds his lover's lifeless hand, closing his eyes and giving in to the exhaustion of his limbs. As the ocean claims Nalini's corpse, D'Kele is determined that it will claim him too.

But a different fate is written in the stars, even though he attempts to deny it. D'Kele's lungs begin to fill with water and he loses consciousness. Nalini's fingers slip free of his grasp, and the two of them are pulled apart. The star-catcher floats back up to the surface, where he is rescued by a Dutch schooner that comes sailing by. When D'Kele is revived, coughing up several pints of salt water, he realizes what has happened and tries to throw himself overboard again. But the crew of the schooner pin him down and tie his hands and legs so he cannot move. The next morning, when they anchor off Prithvideep, the young man is taken ashore and returned to his parents.

Distraught and desperate, D'Kele swears he cannot live without Nalini and begs his mother and father to let him swim out to sea again. They wisely keep him tied to his bed. On the second day, D'Kele lies there weeping. All he can think of is Nalini's lifeless body gliding into the cold embrace of the sea. He barely notices a rustling in the thatched walls of the hut. But then, in front of him, he sees a vision. Nalini stands at the foot of his bed.

She looks at him with a calm, untroubled face. Her eyes are open, and one of her hands reaches out to touch the knots that bind her lover's wrists. She does not loosen the rope but strokes the raw and blistered skin where D'Kele has struggled to break free.

As the star-catcher stares at her in disbelief, not knowing if he is dreaming or if he has awakened out of a nightmare, Nalini turns aside and disappears. The bereaved lover cries out again. For several minutes he is tormented by the lost vision, until she reappears. This time Nalini stands at his side and brushes her fingers through his hair. For the first time since her death, he hears Nalini's voice, a low murmur. The words are indistinct. Yet the sound of her voice soothes him.

Until this time there have been no phantoms on Prithvideep, but soon after the epidemic, others are seen. Not everyone who dies returns as a ghost. Most are gone forever, their souls carried away with their mortal remains. But some revisit the islands—a young boy named Diego, an only child, whose parents find him playing in the sand, three days after they consign his body to the sea. Another ghost is reported on the easternmost island, an old woman who used to live alone with a pet mynah that repeated whatever she said. After the woman dies, the bird refuses to leave the guava tree outside her hut, and the islanders are surprised to hear it begin to speak again, though they cannot decipher its words. One of the old woman's relatives tries to put the mynah in a cage, luring it with bread crumbs. As the bird flies up to a higher branch, the image of the woman appears. After this, others see the phantom and hear her speaking gibberish to the mynah, who echoes every word.

As for D'Kele, he is also stricken by the fever and dies a few weeks after Nalini. Her spirit keeps a vigil by his bed, and after he breathes his last, she watches his parents lay his body on a bier of palm fronds and let the tide take D'Kele out to sea. She does not follow him, but stands alone at the point where the sand is creased by the highest wave. Her face is impassive. As the other mourners depart, they wonder whether she is going to disappear now that her lover is gone. But Nalini knows that D'Kele will return, and by the next morning, when the tide has completed its cycle and the sun has risen, he walks toward her on the beach. For the first time since she slipped from his grasp, they can finally touch each other again.

Over the years, the islanders grow accustomed to the presence of the arora. The phantoms of Prithvideep no longer frighten them. D'Kele and Nalini are often seen together, standing side by side, where the star-catcher once spread his bark cloth scrolls on the beach.

The romance of these two lovers, separated by death but united in the afterlife, becomes one of the favorite stories on the islands. It is recounted again and again. Of all the ghosts on Prithvideep, D'Kele and Nalini are the best known and most loved of the arora. For more than two centuries their spirits inhabit the islands. If they are not seen for more than a day or two, the islanders grow anxious, and it is considered an omen of storms or other catastrophes. When the ghosts reappear, they are greeted with jubilation. Songs and poems are composed in their honor, and when the first street is built on the biggest island, it is named Nalini et D'Kele Avenue. On the anniversary of D'Kele's death, a festival is held on the island, celebrating their love. As a token of good luck, many of the islanders name their children Nalini or D'Kele. Soon after independence, the first president of the Republic has a statue of the two lovers cast in bronze so that they will always watch over the islands. And when the first currency notes are printed on Ilhas dos Fantasmas, replacing the feather money that has been used until then, Nalini's and D'Kele's profiles appear as a watermark on the one-pound note.

But there are other predictions in the night sky that D'Kele has never revealed. He knows that he and Nalini will be separated again. Another tragedy will strike, a crisis as devastating as the epidemic of 1729. For Nalini and D'Kele, it means that once again they will be torn apart from each other, their love divided. On Ilhas dos Fantasmas, it is known as the Great Vanishing of 1932, or the Final Extinction of Arora, when all of the ghosts on the islands disappear.

15

The old Osgood House stood at the corner of Harbor Road and Longfellow Street, not far from the library and the center of Carville. The peaked roofs sloped up at sharp angles, and there was a widow's watch that looked out over the sea. The house had been built in 1879 by a wealthy sea captain, who made his fortune in the East India trade. Carville had older buildings, dating back to colonial times, but the ornate Victorian, with its wraparound porch, arched windows, and fretted gables, was one of the most imposing landmarks in the town.

Hezekiah Osgood bought the house in 1933, when he returned after completing his research. He lived there for the remainder of his life. Very little had changed since his death. The exterior was still painted a dull, grim gray, with the windows and trim picked out in white. An aged dogwood tree grew in front, leaning away from the ocean, stooped by decades of nor'easter storms that blew across Hornswoggle Bay. In 1982, when Hezekiah Osgood died, the house was sold to a mortician.

Alma Parker drove past it every day on her way to work. She had been inside the old Victorian several times to attend wakes and funerals. The porch opened into a large foyer that was empty, except for two porcelain vases filled with silk flowers and a desk where mourners signed their names in the condolence book. A staircase ascended to the second floor, but Alma had never been up there. Overlooking the landing on the stairs was a circular stained glass window with the emblem of a winged conch shell.

There were two large rooms downstairs for viewing the dead, and Alma had often wondered which of these had been the dining room and which was the living room. Most of the original furnishings had been removed, and the wallpaper was a neutral green. The shaded lights were always dimmed.

Growing up as a child in Carville, Alma had heard all kinds of stories about the Osgoods. There were rumors that the family had lived among cannibals and adopted those practices themselves. The Learned Society for the Elucidation of Primitive Cultures had been disbanded soon after Osgood returned, and it was said that he had been practicing black magic and that Clara had been a witch. Nothing was ever proved, but the stories continued even after the professor's death.

Osgood's son, Nicodemus, was the opposite of his father. Instead of locking himself away in a mysterious house, he lived on a fishing boat in the harbor. He was a friendly, outgoing man who greeted everyone he passed. Most of his days were spent behind the counter at Nick's Bait and Tackle Shop, trading stories with other fishermen. He didn't seem to have much time for his father and stayed away from the Victorian house. Alma could still recall the day he came to library, about a week after his father's funeral, and donated all of the professor's books. She was an assistant librarian back then, just out of college. The collection filled almost fifty boxes, and it took months for her to catalog the books, and put them on the shelves. Nick had also given $10,000 of his father's money to the library, though he himself had never once checked out a book.

Driving past the Osgood house, Alma continued down Harbor Street to the center of town, then took a left onto Church Road and left again onto Hyslop Lane, at the end of which she came to the Hornswoggle Bay Nursing Home. Visiting hours were 10:00 to 12:00, and the woman behind the desk smiled when Alma asked if she could see Nick Osgood.

"I'm sure he'll be happy to have some company. Nick doesn't get many visitors," said the receptionist. "His room is down the hall. Number twenty-eight."

"Thank you," said Alma.

"But I have to warn you," the receptionist continued. "Nick doesn't talk very much, and when he does, nobody can understand him."

"That's all right. I just want to say hello."

Though the nursing home had a sterile atmosphere, it was brightly lit and seemed a comfortable place to live if you were old and frail. When Alma reached Room 28, she checked the bag she was carrying to make sure it contained the library books.

On entering the room, Alma heard a plinking sound that made her think of a child's xylophone, a simple, playful tune. At first she couldn't see where the music was coming from, but then she noticed the stooped figure seated in a wheelchair with a strange-looking instrument in his hands.

"Good afternoon, Mr. Osgood. I don't know if you remember me. I'm Alma Parker from the library."

The old man stopped playing and looked up at her with a lost expression in his eyes. As he turned his head, Alma noticed the tattoo on his cheek, the same symbol of the conch shell with wings.

"I hope I'm not disturbing you," she said.

His lips quivered and he stretched out his hand for her to shake. Nick Osgood's fingers may have been thin, but his grip was still firm. He spoke a couple of words that sounded like a foreign language, but nothing that Alma recognized.

"I've been reading your father's book," she said, taking the heavy green volume out of the bag and holding it up for him to see. The old man did not respond, except for a mumbled phrase that made no sense.

"I wish you could tell me how much of this is true," said Alma. "Strange things have been happening at the library, and I'm trying to figure out what's going on."

Nick Osgood seemed to drift back into his own world. His fingers returned to the metal keys of the thumb piano, and he played a couple of notes. Alma took a deep breath and reached into the book bag again, taking out *A Comprehensive History of American Whaling Vessels*.

"I don't want to frighten you," she said, "but you're probably the only person alive who knows what this is."

Opening the book and holding it in front of Nick, Alma wondered if it was the right thing to do. She didn't want the old man to have a heart attack.

It took a moment for him to focus on the image, but suddenly his shoulders rose and his back stiffened. He stopped playing the thumb piano and stared down at the face before him, the boy with tousled hair. Alma could hear the old man's breathing now, an asthmatic sigh that made her wonder if she should close the book. But then she heard him speak, the same garbled language. To her surprise, a reply came out of the book. Leaning forward, Nick Osgood smiled at the boy and nodded his head. He spoke again, this time in long, elaborate sentences, and Alma could see that the ghost understood. The boy was gesturing with both hands and his eyes were full of excitement. The two of them were like old friends who hadn't seen each other for years. Laughing, Nick plucked a few notes from the thumb piano, and the ghost grinned back at him.

For several minutes Alma stood there listening as Nick Osgood kept talking to the ghost. She couldn't bring herself to interrupt them, but in the end the old man started to get agitated and his voice grew louder. He didn't sound angry, but she could see the frustration in his eyes, and his hands began to shake. Worried that he was going to get too anxious and upset, she slowly closed the book. Immediately, his hand shot out to try to stop her, but Alma stepped back.

"I'm sorry," she said. "Maybe I shouldn't have come. I just wanted to know if you could explain who this is."

The old man blurted out another sentence before slumping back in his wheelchair. His breathing was labored, and he closed his eyes after uttering a single word.

"Arora."

"What did you say?" said Alma, recognizing the word. "Did you say *arora*?"

Nick blinked and opened his eyes, then nodded.

"Arora." He pointed at the book.

Before Alma could say any more, the door opened and a bearded man wearing a white coat walked in. He seemed surprised to find her there but smiled.

"Hello," he said, "I'm Dr. Goldfarb. Are you a family member?"

"No. No," said Alma, flustered as she put the book back in her bag. "Just a friend."

"I'm sure Nick is glad to have a visitor. Maybe I'll go and see some of the other patients, then come back later."

"That's all right. I was just leaving," said Alma, heading toward the door. She glanced at Nick, whose eyes followed her. He spoke again, and this time there was a sadness in his words.

Alma turned to the doctor. "Do you know what language he's speaking?"

"Unfortunately, I don't," he said. "Sometimes this happens with patients who suffer from dementia or Alzheimer's. They fall back into a language they spoke in childhood. I think that's what's happening with Nick. He grew up overseas, on an island somewhere—at least that's what I've been told. Maybe he's speaking their language . . . it's hard to know. We haven't been able to find anyone who can translate what he's saying."

The old man kept staring at Alma, as if he knew that they were talking about him.

"Thank you, Doctor," said Alma. "Good-bye, Nick. I'll come and see you again."

16

Ming and Orion weren't sure if they would be allowed into the library again to find the books they needed for their report. But Ms. Parker was not around, and one of her assistants sat behind the main desk. Marigold Deitz was supposed to meet them at 3:30, but by 4:00 she hadn't shown up, and the two of them started without her. Their computer search didn't turn up anything about Prithvideep or Ilhas dos Fantasmas, but when they checked the old card catalog they found the titles of more than twenty books—everything from an economic history of the islands to a hydrographic study of the Bromeil current.

As they headed down the steps into the basement, Orion looked at Ming nervously.

"Maybe we should have chosen Canada after all," he said. "There aren't any ghosts up there."

"How do you know?" said Ming.

"This place gives me the creeps," said Orion, staring at the rows of stacks stretching from one end of the basement to the other, like a corridor lined with narrow cells. Checking their list of books, they quickly found the first call number and title: DS.K344 *A Field Guide to Birds on the Islands of Prithvideep.* It had a yellow cover with a picture of an albatross on the front.

"Open it," said Ming, handing the book to Orion.

"You open it," he said, shaking his head.

The two of them looked at each other and grinned foolishly, afraid of what they might find inside. At the same moment there was the sound of footsteps on the stairs and Marigold's voice.

"Hello! Anyone there?"

"You're late," said Ming.

"Sorry, I had to get my hair straightened after school," said Marigold. "I also went to the tanning salon. Can you tell the difference?"

She held out both arms for them to see.

"Whatever," said Orion.

"Did you find out anything about your islands," asked Marigold, "or should we choose another country?"

"There's plenty of information here," said Ming. "We just got this book."

Marigold took the yellow book from her and glanced at the cover with a disinterested look.

"A bird book? That's all you've found?"

"We just started. There's a bunch of other books too," said Ming.

Marigold shrugged and opened the field guide to a page with pictures of different species of ducks. Orion and Ming took a step closer. There didn't seem to be anything hiding inside the book. On the next page was a map of the Indian Ocean with the migratory routes of birds that wintered on the islands, some of them flying all the way from Russia and Central Asia.

"Boring," said Marigold, running a finger through her hair. With a distracted gesture, she flipped over a couple more pages, then stopped abruptly. Her eyes opened wide and her skin paled, even though she'd just been to the tanning salon. With a shrill, choked scream, Marigold hurled the book on the ground. Her hair, which had been straight a few seconds earlier, frizzed out at the ends. In a panic, Marigold turned and ran back up the stairs.

"I don't think that was a picture of a bird," said Ming after Marigold had left. "Let's take a look."

Cautiously, Orion picked up the book. They pried the pages open again, and a hideous face confronted them—a man with a festering scar that ran from the middle of his forehead to the bridge of his nose, across one eye and down his cheek. It looked as if his head had been cut in half and glued back together again. Instead of a right eye, there was nothing but an oozing scab. The left eye made up for the one that was missing with a malevolent glare. This was clearly not a pleasant ghost. The image smeared the surface of the page, like an oil slick on water. Strands of greasy hair hung down from the man's balding scalp, which was crawling with lice. Both of his ears were pierced with rusty fishhooks, as if the lobes were bait. His beard grew in patches, the texture and color of an old scouring brush used to clean the deck of a ship. His moustache was flecked with fish scales and bits of seaweed. Around the ghost's neck hung a chain of shark's teeth. His lips were cracked and bleeding, and the few teeth in his mouth were yellow stubs protruding out of rotting gums. As Orion and Ming watched in horror, the ghost raised one sleeve and wiped his nose. Then he licked his lips with a gray tongue that emerged from his mouth like a clam coming out of its shell.

Ming put one hand over her mouth, as if she were going to throw up. Orion was also grimacing with disgust, holding the book as far away from himself as possible.

When the ghost began to speak, he was even more revolting. The spirit cursed them in his own language—strange words and syllables that sounded as ugly and terrifying as he looked. After a volley of abuse, he gave a hoarse laugh that snorted out through his nose. The grotesque wheezing ended in a coughing fit, and Ming could almost feel the spittle flying off the page as the ghost hacked and gagged.

"I don't think we need this book for our report," said Orion, snapping it shut.

"Wait," said Ming. "There must be others. Let's get the rest of the books on our list and see what we find."

"Where do you think Marigold went?"

"I don't know, but I'm sure she's not coming back."

It took the two of them half an hour to find all the books, which they stacked on the desk at the end of the aisle. Looking up at the window overhead, Orion wished he had never climbed into the library two nights before.

"Okay," Ming said, "we'll do this one by one. I'll open the first book, then you can do the next. Let's see how many ghosts we can find."

Only a third of the books had spirits tucked between the pages, and none were as frightening as the first ghost they'd found. There was one old woman with matted white hair who kept wailing and wringing her hands, but most of the spirits looked like ordinary people. Several of them were children who seemed lost or abandoned. The ghosts appeared to come from different parts of the world—some were African, others Asian or European. They were dressed in a variety of clothes, naval uniforms and Victorian gowns, embroidered caftans and simple loincloths. One of the ghosts wore a turban and was smoking a water pipe with a long coiled stem. Some of the spirits gestured and spoke, while others were silent, blinking their eyes and biting their lips. From the expressions on their faces it was clear that all of the ghosts could see Ming and Orion.

"I wish we could understand what they were saying," said Ming. "I wish we could answer them."

By now they had almost finished searching through the pile of books. Orion picked up a large, leather-bound volume, the title printed in gold lettering: *A Genealogy of Ilhas dos Fantasmas*. Inside he found diagrams of family trees and lists of names, with dates of births and deaths. There were also a few pictures, reproductions of old portraits, and several black-and-white photographs of important people from Prithvideep. Compared to the ghosts, these images looked two-dimensional.

One of the pictures caught Orion's eye.

"Look," he said. "Isn't that the man who was smoking the pipe?"

" 'Sheikh Rustom Ibn Fanous al Ifrit.' " Ming read his name slowly, not sure if she was pronouncing it correctly.

They quickly found the book containing his ghost and compared the two images. It was definitely the same man, though the portrait was poorly printed and not very clear, while the apparition on the page was completely lifelike. The turbaned figure eyed them with a dignified expression. When he put the mouthpiece of the pipe to his lips, they could hear a gentle, gurgling sound.

17

Sheikh Rustom Ibn Fanous al Ifrit studies the two faces staring at him and wonders where these children have come from. They appear out of nowhere and seem to hover overhead like genies let out of a bottle.

He tries to recall how long he has been held captive inside the book, but there is no way for him to measure the years and months that have passed. The sheikh understands that unlike in the mortal world, where time is calculated with precision and everything has a clear beginning and end, in the spirit world, he and the other ghosts live a fluid existence without any definite sense of past or present. Though born in 1661, he has no idea what century it is right now. Time melts away and nothing changes. Sheikh Rustom's beard is just as gray as it was on the day of his death, his fingernails have grown no longer, his turban remains perfectly pleated, and his water pipe never goes out. Though he feels no urgency or impatience to escape, he often wishes that he could tear himself free from the restrictive bindings of the book.

For most of his life, the sheikh has been a sailor, and his fondest memories are a sequence of departures and arrivals. His wooden dhow, with its cedar hull and canvas sail, carries him across the seven seas, from the coastline of Africa to the rim of Cathay. Like the legendary Sinbad, he sets sail from Arabian ports and explores every corner of the globe. Sheikh Rustom trades in silks and saffron, frankincense and precious stones. He serves as an emissary to the courts of India and Europe. His dhow transports eminent passengers and precious cargo—from a Catalan philosopher to the golden feathers of a phoenix. He survives the most violent storms, hurricanes, and typhoons. He safely pilots his ship through the narrowest straits and between treacherous icebergs. His anchor is lowered at the luxurious ports of Venice and Alexandria as well as on deserted islands, where nothing can be found but sand and flies. His life is a series of voyages, measured only from the moment the ropes slip free of the dock until the first smudge of distant shores appears in his spyglass. Being a sailor, all that he cares about are the countless days between, the salt spray of the sea, the stars to guide him at night, waves jostling the horizon, dolphins keeping pace with his dhow.

Eventually, fate carries him to Prithvideep and wrecks his ship during an equinoctial storm. The hull of the dhow splinters against the reef. Sheikh Rustom is flung into the turbulent surf. The rest of his crew are drowned, but he washes ashore and chooses to settle on Ilhas dos Fantasmas. Though he sometimes feels an urge to set sail again, the islands seem to hold him in their spell, as if he has reached a final destination. He builds a house for himself, gets married, and fathers seven children. Sheikh Rustom trades with ships from every continent and becomes one of the most powerful men in Prithvideep. After his death in the epidemic of 1729, he returns to the islands as an arora and watches over his family and friends until the moment he disappears in the Great Vanishing. Sheikh Rustom recalls a strange stooped figure with a black hood over his head and one protruding eye. That is the last thing he remembers, except for a blinding explosion. He feels himself sucked into that eye, as if it were a funnel of light.

From that moment onward, he lives within the book, confined to the page like a jellyfish stranded upon the shore. He knows it is a book because of the words that enclose him, the printed lines of letters that cage him in on either side. Sheikh Rustom has seen many strange and mysterious things in his travels and encountered the most dangerous enemies. He has been captured by pirates and imprisoned in desolate forts, but never has he known this form of incarceration—a dungeon of ink and paper. His instincts tell him that he is trapped under the spell of an evil magician, a cruel sorcerer who hides his face behind a black veil.

All of this happens many years ago. Now he sees the curious faces of two children peering down at him. The arora of Sheikh Rustom Ibn Fanous al Ifrit does not recognize them, though he can tell they mean him no harm. As he smokes his pipe and contemplates his circumstances, the children seem to be watching him through a lens of history, a refraction of time. It almost seems as if they are looking at one another through opposite ends of an empty hourglass.

18

Courtney was still grounded, but her mother had gone out shopping. When Ming and Orion arrived at the house, Agnes greeted the two friends as if she hadn't seen them in years, wagging her shaggy tail and whimpering with excitement.

"You've got to come with us," said Ming.

"I can't," said Courtney. "If my mom comes home and finds me gone, I'm dead."

"But we found a lot more ghosts," said Orion. "The library is full of them."

"Marigold Deitz saw one and nearly fainted. It was this gross-looking man, with a scar across his face—"

Courtney interrupted Ming, her eyes wide with alarm.

"If Marigold knows, that means everybody is going to find out."

"What should we do?" said Orion, puffing out his cheeks in frustration.

"I don't know," said Courtney. "Right now the ghosts are all inside the books, but if they get out, who knows what will happen. Maybe we should warn Ms. Parker."

"She wasn't at the library this afternoon." Ming frowned, not sure how Ms. Parker would react.

"I know where she lives," said Orion. "On Larch Street, near the fire station."

"I don't think she's going to believe us," said Ming.

"She may already know," said Courtney. "The way she looked at us yesterday, I think she has suspicions."

"Then we should go right now," said Ming, nodding slowly as she realized they had no choice.

"What time is it?" asked Courtney.

"Five thirty," said Orion.

"My mom won't be back for another hour. I'll come with you. Just wait a second."

Courtney ran upstairs and grabbed her backpack. A few minutes later the three of them were racing down the street on their bicycles as if they were being chased by ghosts. They flew down the hills and spun around corners, taking every shortcut they could find until they reached Larch Street, where they stopped, out of breath.

"I hope we're doing the right thing," said Orion. "It's the green house on the right."

Courtney rang the bell, and all three of them waited anxiously until the door opened. Ted Parker greeted them with a friendly frown.

"If you're selling magazine subscriptions, we aren't interested," he said.

"Is Ms. Parker home?"

"She's just finishing supper. Can you come back later?"

"It's really important," said Courtney. "It's . . . it's a matter of life and death."

Ted Parker raised his eyebrows, then stood aside to let the three of them into the house. He called to his wife, who appeared a minute later with a paper napkin in one hand. When Alma saw who it was, she nodded and led them into the living room.

"Maybe you could clear the table, Ted," she said. "Please. I'll deal with this."

"We're sorry to bother you, Ms. Parker, but there's something serious happening at the library," Courtney began to explain.

"Tell me exactly what you've found," said Alma.

Taking the book out of her backpack, Courtney handed it over. The librarian opened the pages cautiously and saw the woman inside, her mournful eyes and long dark hair, a coral necklace around her throat. The image was just like the one from the other book, a pale meniscus of yellowish light covering the page.

"We found a lot more like this," said Ming. "In other books. All of them are different."

"Yes, I've seen one too," said Alma.

"They're ghosts," said Orion. "We summoned them from the dead."

"When was this?" Alma looked at him sternly.

"Two nights ago, when we sneaked into the stacks," said Courtney, looking at the floor. "There was an incantation in that big green book, and we said the words together. We didn't really think it would work, calling up ghosts."

"They're known as arora," said the librarian. "They used to live on Ilhas dos Fantasmas."

"Yes, we read about that, but what are they doing *here*?" asked Ming.

"I'm not completely sure," said Alma, "but somehow they were trapped inside these books."

"Why didn't anyone find them before?" Orion asked.

"Because they must have been invisible before we repeated the incantation," said Courtney.

"Is there any way to get them out?" Ming asked.

"I hope so," said the librarian. "Does anybody else know about this?"

Orion and Ming told her what had happened with Marigold Deitz.

"All right. I'm going to need your help," said Alma. "Where are the books you took out today?"

"We put them back on the shelves, but here's a list," said Ming, handing her a folded piece of paper.

"Good. Can you come to the library tomorrow, after school? We're going to have to do some research."

"Sure," said Ming.

"Yeah," said Orion.

"I'll try," said Courtney. "But I'm grounded."

Alma glanced down at the image of the woman. "I'll hold on to this book. Thank you for coming by."

After she let the three of them out the door, Alma turned and called to her husband.

"Ted, can you come in here, please? I think you need to take a look at this."

19

Marigold Deitz had told her parents what had happened. She claimed she'd seen some kind of horrible, slimy creature, though she wasn't sure what it was. Her mother had phoned Mr. Abernathy, the principal, who phoned Marigold's homeroom teacher.

The next morning, Alma Parker got a call from Roberta Hokum saying that one of her students was very upset with what she'd found in a library book.

"Do you know which book it was?" asked Alma.

"A bird book," said Roberta.

"That doesn't sound very dangerous. What exactly did she see?"

"I can't say," Roberta replied in an irritated tone. "But it was definitely something ugly and offensive. I think you should close the library until we discover what it is."

"Do you really think that's necessary?" said Alma.

"It's a matter of public safety. The books should all be quarantined." Mrs. Hokum's voice grew sharper, more demanding.

"Was your student injured in any way?"

"No, but she's very frightened."

"Well, I'll certainly investigate," said Alma. "But we can't close the library just because someone got scared."

"I don't think you're taking this seriously enough," said the teacher, each word edged with accusation.

"Don't worry, Roberta. I'm taking it very seriously. You can be sure of that."

After speaking to Alma Parker, Mrs. Hokum went to the gym, where her sixth-grade class was having PE. She interrupted a game of badminton that Ming and Orion were playing and made them come back to the classroom.

"I want to know exactly what happened at the library," demanded Mrs. Hokum. "What did you do to Marigold?"

"We didn't do anything," said Ming.

"I don't believe you," said their teacher. "Her mother says she's very upset. You must have played some sort of trick on her."

"No," said Orion. "She just opened a book and started to scream."

"What was inside the book?" said Mrs. Hokum, her lips tightening like a pink rubber band.

Ming and Orion looked at each other helplessly.

"Nothing really . . . ," said Ming, trying to think of some way to get out of revealing the truth without lying.

"Don't play games with me, young lady!" Mrs. Hokum snarled through a clenched line of perfectly white teeth.

"We're really not sure what it is, but . . ." Orion trailed off.

Mrs. Hokum's eyes were instruments of torture, forcing him to tell the truth. He swallowed hard.

"It was a ghost," blurted Orion. "A horrible man with fish-hooks in his ears and a scar across his face."

Ming was about to jump in when she noticed the angry disbelief in her teacher's expression.

"Do you think this is some kind of joke?" said Mrs. Hokum.

"No. It's true," said Orion. "The ghosts are from Ilhas dos Fantasmas. Most of them aren't dangerous at all. They're trapped inside the books. We found them while we were researching our report for the World's Fair."

"I don't like it when my students tell lies," said Mrs. Hokum. "How can you expect me to believe what you're saying? Now I want an explanation."

"Please, Mrs. Hokum," said Ming, realizing that the more they insisted it was true, the more she'd distrust them. "He's not lying. And we didn't try to scare Marigold."

Their teacher shook her head impatiently.

"That's enough," she said. "If you're going to be stubborn and dishonest, I'll have to send a note home to your parents. I don't know what games the two of you are playing, but you can be sure you're not going to do a report on this so-called Island of Phantoms. I'll choose another country for you instead."

"But we need to find out how the ghosts got into the library," said Orion.

"Stop it," said Mrs. Hokum sharply. "I don't want to hear any more talk about ghosts. Is that clear?"

20

By the time Ming and Orion got to the library, Ms. Parker had already located a number of books and articles related to Ilhas dos Fantasmas. She gave them each a list of references—titles, dates, page numbers—and asked them to search for anything that might hold a clue to the secret of the arora.

"Ms. Parker," said Ming hesitantly. "This morning we had to tell Mrs. Hokum about the ghosts. She wanted to know why Marigold got scared, but when we told her, she didn't believe us."

"Hopefully that will be the end of it," Alma said with a frown. "Have either of you told your parents?"

Orion and Ming exchanged guilty glances and shook their heads.

"That would probably be a good idea," said Alma. "I don't want you getting into trouble because of this."

"My parents would never believe me," said Ming with a helpless shrug.

"Mine would probably send me to a psychiatrist," Orion added. "They already think I'm crazy."

"Then maybe I should give them a call once I figure out what's going on." said Alma. "Anyway, let's get to work, and please be careful. So far the ghosts have been harmless, but we can't be sure . . ."

Several of the books in the Osgood collection were written in languages other than English, including a Portuguese chronicle of the islands—*Historia de Ilhas dos Fantasmas*—and a medical treatise—*Maladies Tropicales*—by a French doctor who spent several years on Prithvideep. There was also a book in German by a Professor Dieter Von Claptrapp—*Das Alta Licht von den Sternen*. Alma wasn't able to read any of it, though there were a number of charts and diagrams that looked as if they had something to do with astronomy. There were also a few black-and-white illustrations, line drawings in which the figures of islanders were shown peeling bark off of trees and making some kind of parchment. As she turned the pages, Alma came upon a folded sheet of paper tucked inside the book. It was covered in notes, and she recognized Hezekiah Osgood's handwriting, the spidery blue lines of ink from a fountain pen. He had translated a few passages and added his own comments alongside.

Complete analysis of the optical properties of
Glutinous luminosa, a rare species of gum tree found
only on these islands
Properties: exudes a clear resin that absorbs starlight
sensitive only to sidereal light (illumination from
the stars)
Star-Catchers—they peel the bark from these trees,

form it into large sheets of paper (more like coarse cloth). These are laid out on the beach at night (moonless) for several hours, then collected and rolled into scrolls—an ancient tradition, accompanied by incantations, etc.

Results in patterns of light on the bark-cloth
Traces the movement of stars, imprinted on the surface
      kept as scrolls, sacred tradition
Some say they can read the future in these patterns
Note: I have examined several of these Star Cloths, which provide a clear and unambiguous image of the night sky—a remarkable phenomenon for which I can offer no scientific explanation at this time. There are several Star-Catchers still living on these islands who continue to practice their magical art, and one or two groves of gum trees are protected, exclusively for their use.

      * May work in emulsion for photographing arora

This was all there was, a few cryptic lines scrawled in blue ink. Hezekiah Osgood had written nothing more, and the German book offered no more answers, except for the black-and-white illustrations and several examples of star patterns, a series of concentric arcs, formed by the rotation of the Earth.

As Ming and Orion searched through each of the bound volumes of magazines and books, Alma carefully compiled a bibliography of sources.

Fleisch, D.K. "Prithvideep: The Tropical Isle of Phantoms."
National Geographic. Vol. 172, No. 3
(September 1981) pp. 289–295.

Back issues of *National Geographic* filled a dozen shelves in the stacks, going back to 1928, when the library first started its subscription. Some of the issues had gone missing, and a couple of volumes were out of place, but Orion didn't have any trouble locating the article.

From the photographs, Prithvideep looked like any other tropical island, with golden sand and coral reefs. There were pictures of hammocks under palm trees and snorkelers peering at lionfish through diving masks. The colors were bright and vivid, especially the blue of the ocean and sky. One photograph showed a panorama of the main town, which had grown up around the waterfront. None of the buildings were more than two stories high, and there were only a dozen streets. In 1981, when the article was published, there were only twelve cars on the islands, and the farthest you could drive was two miles in any direction. One of the smaller islands had been turned into a resort hotel, with thatch cottages surrounding an idyllic lagoon. It looked like the perfect place to take a vacation.

The article was also illustrated with a couple of black-and-white photographs from the 1920s that depicted an earlier era when the waterfront was nothing but a line of rusty sheds. A second picture, in sepia tones, showed the president of the Republic greeting a delegation of visitors. In the fine print of the caption, Orion found Hezekiah Osgood's name. He was standing to the left of the president—a tall gaunt man with a graying beard. Of all the faces in the picture, his was the only one looking directly at the camera, and Orion felt as if he were staring straight at him.

Though the title of the article referred to "The Isle of Phantoms," there was only a brief reference to ghosts. The *National Geographic* writer dismissed the stories of spirits as "quaint superstitions and folklore." He went on to say that some of the older residents of the islands claimed there had been a time when ghosts were commonly seen and recognized. But that had changed in 1932, when the ghosts had suddenly disappeared. The article continued:

> This is sometimes called "the Great Extinction," which is supposed to make us think that ghosts and phantoms have disappeared like the dodo bird or the passenger pigeon. Some have even suggested that ghosts are subject to a process of supernatural selection—a fanciful idea without any supporting scientific evidence.

There was also a passing reference to the star-catchers, whom the author dismissed as "primitive astrologers whose rituals have faded into obscurity since the gum trees they once used to produce bark cloth have all been destroyed."

Much of the article focused on recent developments. Modern technology had arrived in Prithvideep, including a small airfield, telephone connections, and satellite TV. The writer had spent most of his time at the resort hotel, enjoying cuttlefish curry and a coconut oil massage.

The only other mention of ghosts accompanied the last photograph, which was taken in the main square of the capital and showed a statue of two figures cast in bronze. The caption read: "D'Kele and Nalini: Prithvideep's own Romeo and Juliet, who haunt these islands with their eternal love." Studying the picture, Orion couldn't help but recognize the arora Courtney had found.

Agrimwich, M. I. "Scholar Returns from Indian Ocean." *Hornswoggle Gazette*. April 16, 1933. p. 1.

A photograph of Hezekiah Osgood filled most of the front page of the *Hornswoggle Gazette*. Ming didn't like the look in his eyes, a shrewd glare. The article described a reception held in his honor by the Learned Society for the Elucidation of Primitive Cultures. There wasn't much information about Osgood or Prithvideep, mostly quotes from speeches made by other members of the society, who praised the professor for his "diligent pursuit of knowledge and admirable efforts to spread the benefits of puritan values among savage peoples." In the last paragraph of the article, the reporter explained that the professor had returned home with twenty steamer trunks full of books, artifacts, and papers.

Gris, Lee. "Controversial Magic-Lantern Lecture on Far-Flung Lands." *The Boston Herald American*. December 2, 1934. Evening edition, p. 6.

Ming had some trouble finding this article because it had been clipped out of the newspaper and filed away in a folder marked CARVILLE HISTORICAL SOCIETY. Hezekiah Osgood had been invited to give a talk about his research at the Boston Atheneum. According to some of the members quoted by the reporter, the professor caused an uproar by suggesting that he had actually encountered ancestral spirits on the islands of Prithvideep. "Total bunk!" said one of the Atheneum's distinguished members. "The worst kind of scholarly hogwash!" said another. "A disgrace," said a third, "that an institution like ours, devoted to philosophical and scientific integrity, should have to endure the false claims and fabrications of an academic huckster." The only member of the Atheneum who seemed to have anything positive to say about the lecture was a man named Clarence Beasley: "Though I do not accept any of his conclusions, Professor Osgood did accompany his lecture with a magic-lantern show, which revealed some fascinating photographs that he claims are images from the afterlife." These were projected onto a screen and seemed to move, like a cinematic film. Several of those who attended the lecture were quoted as saying it was a hoax, "nothing but a lot of smoke and mirrors."

"Wife of Reclusive Scholar Who Accompanied Him to the East." Obituary. *Carville Gazette.* January 22, 1951, p. 8.

Clara Osgood was described as a devoted companion and outspoken supporter of her husband's work. While Professor Osgood retreated into isolation after his theories met with derision and ridicule, Clara Osgood defended her husband whenever possible. The photograph that accompanied her obituary revealed a pale, severe-looking woman with her hair pulled back from her face and a lace bonnet perched on her head. When Orion first looked at the picture, he felt a shiver go up both arms, as if Mrs. Osgood's eyes were following him. The obituary went on to say that she had been an active member of the Daughters of the American Revolution and the Hornswoggle Temperance Society. She died at the age of 71, after a brief illness. The only surviving family members were Professor Osgood and their son, Nicodemus.

Greusholm, T.V. "LSEPC Closes Down." *Boston Globe*. March 10, 1953. City edition, p. 24C.

The Learned Society for the Elucidation of Primitive Cultures, which used to be one of the most respected scholarly institutions in the country, has disbanded. The LSEPC president, Dr. Marcus D'Oench announced the closing today, and said that the society faced insurmountable questions of credibility. Most of the blame lay with Prof. Hezekiah T. Osgood, a founding member and past president of the society, "whose theories on phantasmagoric-optical phenomena and necrophotomimesis have irreversibly disgraced and divided our membership.

Ming wasn't sure what all these words meant, but she knew it wasn't any ordinary kind of science. The article went on to explain that Osgood's research had been discounted by eminent scholars at Harvard and MIT. Even in his own hometown he faced suspicion and hostility from those who believed he was engaged in black magic. One of his neighbors, Mrs. Flora Ibsen, was quoted as saying, "He's a very strange man and we don't know what goes on in that house, except it must be some kind of evil, that's for sure." Even Osgood's own son was estranged from his father, though he refused to be interviewed for the article. Professor Osgood himself was also unavailable for comment.

Osgood, Hezekiah T. "Phantasmaoptical Phenomenon and Necrophotomimesis." *Journal of the Learned Society for the Elucidation of Primitive Cultures.* Vol. 6. Winter, 1938, pp. 723–746.

The LSEPC journals had been moved out of the stacks and put in the library's attic, where books and papers were kept that nobody ever looked at but that were considered too important to throw away. After some searching, Alma was able to find the dusty boxes and dig out the issue containing Osgood's article.

The pages had yellowed and were so fragile that Alma decided to make a photocopy before reading it. Fortunately, the machine was working, though it groaned miserably. Osgood's article began with a brief introduction:

> Modern technology has fostered a greater understanding of the natural world, with increasingly powerful microscopes that explore minuscule cells and giant telescopes that reach out to touch the heavens. We have split the atom and developed medicines to cure and prevent the most dreaded diseases. A few years ago, all of this would have

seemed impossible. Why, then, should we not accept the notion that technology can also reveal the marvels and mysteries of the supernatural world? Science has shown how many phenomena, once considered heresy, are now accepted as empirical truths. Man's quest for knowledge, his ingenuity and intellect, have solved the most daunting riddles of the universe. Why, then, should we not open our minds to the possibilities of communicating with the dead?

The professor went on to describe some of his experiences with ghosts on Prithvideep and the experiments that he conducted. He reiterated his theory that the ghosts were composed entirely of light, but that this was a unique form of illumination "projected out of the past."[14] After explaining the technical modifications he had made to his camera and the use of resin from *Glutinous luminosa* as an "optical adhesive," he went on to describe how he had been able to capture images of the arora and transfer these from photographic plates to paper. The process, which he called necrophotomimesis, was accomplished using a simple magic-lantern projector, through which he focused the light onto blank sheets of paper or the pages of books. Once the image was projected onto the page, it was fixed there with a coating of resin.[15]

---

14. Each arora possesses its own particular illumination, or "arrested evanescence," as Osgood termed it.

15. Osgood coined the expression "sticky light" to describe the process by which the arora are transferred from a glass negative onto the page of a book. The resin from the gum trees allows the images to stick to paper or any other dry, flat surface. Once projected into a book, there seemed to be no method of removing the arora, as if it were permanently fixed to the page.

This is accompanied by certain chants and incantations that I learned from the Necromancers of Prithvideep. These spells facilitate the transfer of light and glue it to the surface. In this way, the arora is preserved in a form that allows for careful and continuous observation, much like specimens in a bottle of formaldehyde.

Osgood also discovered certain incantations that made the spirits invisible once they were stuck to the page. The professor provided a detailed report on the early stages of his research, which he admitted was a process of trial and error. He conducted many of his first experiments on the Isle of Banished Spirits by mounting his tripod and camera in a small boat and sailing close to the shore. When the evil phantoms glowered and lunged at him, he took their photographs. Many of these images were destroyed because he had not perfected the technology, "and others were so gruesome, I had no choice but to burn them up." Soon, all of the dangerous spirits had been removed from the barren island. By this time Osgood had refined his methods and soon turned his lens on the more gentle arora.

Cree, P. "Ambassador of Island Republic Issues Protest." *New York Times*. City edition, June 15, 1938. p. 33.

After searching through an online periodicals index, Ming turned up an article in the library's microfiche collection. Projecting it onto the monitor screen, she saw it was only a few inches of print, a brief report hidden away in the back pages of the newspaper. The article explained that the ambassador of Prithvideep had submitted a formal complaint to the U.S. government, stating that Osgood had smuggled "objects of great cultural and spiritual value" off of the islands. The government of Prithvideep demanded that these be returned. However, the professor had responded by saying that he had brought with him "nothing more than my own books and papers." While the U.S. State Department investigated the claim, no charges were brought because the ambassador refused to state exactly what objects had been stolen.

When Ming showed the article to Ms. Parker, the librarian read it carefully, her face clouded with concern. Though it still wasn't clear exactly what was going on in the library, Alma realized there were a lot more secrets hidden in Professor Osgood's collection.

21

Once you've seen a ghost, everything around you looks a little bit different. The sunlight seems to change, as if it were dusted with pollen; shadows no longer have a hollow emptiness; and every breath of air carries the possibilities of a hidden presence. After helping Ms. Parker with the research, Ming and Orion bicycled over to Rattle Beach, half a mile outside of town, on the eastern edge of Hornswoggle Bay. It was one of their favorite places, where they could sit alone and talk. The beach was not very large, covered with shingle instead of sand and rimmed on both sides with shelves of granite, known as Headstone Point. When they arrived, the tide was just beginning to go out, and waves were lapping against the shore.

The outgoing tide sucked on the loose stones and made a rattling sound—a low rumble, as if a bagful of marbles were being shaken. Headstone Point got its name because years ago, the granite had been quarried to make gravestones. Most of the cemeteries in New England were marked with slabs of gray rock cut from Headstone Point.

"Do you really think those are ghosts inside the books?" said Ming. "Maybe it's just an optical illusion."

"I don't know, they looked real enough to me." Orion shaded his eyes as he stared out at the lobster buoys rocking on the waves.

Later in the summer, Rattle Beach would attract a lot of swimmers and sunbathers, but it was still too cold for anyone to go in the water. A sailboat scudded past, leaning into the wind as it rounded Headstone Point. Everything looked perfectly normal, rumpled clouds on the horizon, yet Orion could tell that something was bothering Ming. She seemed unsettled and uneasy.

"What's up?" he said.

"Nothing, really. . . ."

"C'mon . . . tell me."

"Well, I did something today I probably shouldn't have done," said Ming, looking away.

"Yeah?" said Orion sarcastically. "So, what's new about that?"

"Well . . . while we were searching through the books in the library, I was flipping through one, and a letter fell out. It had a really cool stamp on it, and I don't know why . . . but I put it in my pocket. I probably should have given it to Ms. Parker, but somehow I didn't think it was that important."

"So?"

"Afterwards, I looked at it more carefully. The letter is from Professor Osgood, and it's never been opened."

Ming reached into her pocket and took out a long rectangular envelope made of heavy cream-colored paper. The stamp in the upper right-hand corner was from Ilhas dos Fantasmas. It had a picture of a tropical fish with brilliant colors, all red and yellow, with speckles of blue. The addresses on the envelope were written neatly with blue ink in an elliptical, cursive hand.

From:
Professor Hezekiah T. Osgood
PO Box 26
Ilhas dos Fantasmas (Prithvideep)

> *To: M. Edouard Isidore Buguet*
> *Occult Photographer*
> *Blvd. Montmarte*
> *Paris, France*

The envelope was covered with a number of black cancellation marks, and across the front was written:

Décédé. Rétourné à l'expenditeur.

"What does that mean?" said Orion, puzzled.

"Deceased. Return to Sender," said Ming, who had looked up the words in a French-English dictionary while she was at the library.

Turning the letter over, Orion could see it was sealed.

"So what should we do with it?" asked Ming.

"I think you should just put this letter back where you found it and forget about it," said Orion.

"Are you crazy?" said Ming. "We've got to find out what's going on. Maybe this letter will tell us. We've got to open it."

"Forget it." Orion glared at Ming accusingly; she'd gotten him into enough trouble already.

By now the tide had dropped, and more of the shoreline had been exposed, long fingers of kelp-covered granite stretching into the sea. The rocks where the two of them were sitting had been cut into long squares and rectangles. Just thinking about the gravestones that came from Headstone Point made Orion feel uncomfortable. He could imagine the granite being quarried, polished, and inscribed, *R.I.P.* For a few minutes neither of them spoke, staring out at the hypnotic swell of the ocean.

"I don't care what you think," said Ming, straightening her shoulders. "I'm going to open it."

Orion knew there wasn't any point in arguing with her. He winced as Ming slipped her finger under the flap of the envelope and tore it open.

Inside, there were two sheets of paper folded together. The upper sheet was a letter.

May 6, 1922

Dear M. Buguet,

I am a great admirer of your pioneering work in the field of spirit photography. It is unfortunate that more people do not accept your important discoveries, and those of other visionaries like the late William Mumler. It is high time that the world understood the vital link between the camera and the afterlife.

Though I cannot reveal too much in this letter, certain revelations have come to light here on Ilhas dos Fantasmas, which I believe will convince the world of the scientific basis of occult photography.

If I may be so bold as to trouble you, enclosed is a specimen of one of my recent experiments. I would be honored and delighted to travel to Paris to meet with you and discuss these matters further, at your earliest convenience.

I am sir,
most sincerely yours,
Hezekiah T. Osgood, Ph.D.

Orion wasn't sure if the paper was rustling in Ming's hands because of the sea breeze, or if her fingers were trembling, but when she turned to the next page, he felt a jolt of surprise. Even though they had seen dozens of ghosts in the library books already, Orion still wasn't used to being confronted by an arora. The sheet of writing paper was folded into three sections, and the face that appeared looked as if it were creased as well. The ghost was a young girl, about their age, with her hair in pigtails and a cramped frown on her face. Very carefully, Ming flattened the paper on her lap, and the arora looked grateful. Her eyes were curious and expressive. She lifted both arms over her head and stretched, then waved at Ming and Orion as if it were the most natural thing in the world, to greet someone from another time and place.

22

Though she feels no discomfort after being tucked inside the envelope for so many years, Cziczee is still relieved to find herself unfolded. The glare of sunlight is dazzling, and it takes her eyes a few minutes to adjust after the darkness. She can't remember how long it's been since she saw clouds and the ocean, though the rocky coastline doesn't look at all like the beaches of Prithvideep. Cziczee doesn't recognize the two children who stare at her. The clothes they wear are strange and uncomfortable-looking for someone who has always worn a loose cotton shift and gone about barefoot all her life.

Cziczee remembers Professor Osgood and his wife trying to get her to wear shoes, a sunbonnet, and a school uniform. She is one of the only students to enroll in the professor's Latin Grammar Academy. The first school on Prithvideep, it fails because most of the children can't stand the idea of sitting indoors all day and learning useless things like the plural past subjunctive or the rules for diagramming sentences, as well as arithmetic and moral science. Within a year, Osgood closes the school because he himself is much more interested in conducting his experiments on the arora. The only person who shows any interest in education is Cziczee. She convinces Osgood to give her private lessons because she wants to become a teacher. Even though he is a professor, Hezekiah isn't a good teacher. He insists that Cziczee learn Latin.

"Once you learn the Latin names for things like birds," he tells her, "then you'll be able to classify them according to their biological order, family, genus, and species."

This doesn't make much sense to Cziczee. Each of the birds that visit Ilhas dos Fantasmas already has a name. Why should she have to call them something else? Cziczee herself is named after a bird, a tiny finch with gray wings and a purple crest that arrives on the islands in late May. What's the point in calling it *Carpodacus fulvous*? Cziczee birds get their name from the call they make, which sounds like someone whistling through a comb. Cziczee already knows the names of most of the birds that migrate through Prithvideep, like the speckled coral pecker that wades along the reef at low tide, eating crabs and sea slugs. Though everyone on Prithvideep has known about this bird for years, Professor Osgood claims it is a new species that he discovered and names it after himself, *Ploverus osgoodiana*. Cziczee thinks it is the dumbest name she's ever heard, though she doesn't say this to the professor. He also tries to teach her the Latin names for plants and trees, like *Glutinous luminosa*, which everybody knows as the star-catcher tree. He has Latin names for fish and fossils, insects and seashells. In his laboratory, Professor Osgood has collected all kinds of specimens, pickled snakes bottled in alcohol, glass cases full of butterflies stuck on pins, albums bulging with pressed leaves and ferns, all with their names written in Latin.

One day, Cziczee gets so bored with her lessons she wanders off on her own while the professor is working on one of his photographic experiments. Instead of going home, she follows a trail to a rock that overlooks a sheltered cove on the north side of the island. From there she can see two smaller islands covered with breadfruit trees. They look like leafy mushrooms poking out of the waves.

In the distance, she sees a sailing ship disappearing over the horizon. Cziczee wants to leave the islands and travel to some other country, where she can study important, useful things like poetry and physics. She dreams of stowing away on one of the ships that pass through Prithvideep. Once she's learned everything she can about the outside world, Cziczee wants to return to Prithvideep and open a real school, where children will enjoy what they learn.

As Cziczee is sitting on the rock, she can see a storm gathering in the distance. The clouds come racing toward her much faster than the ships that ride the wind. Within minutes, the sun disappears and it looks as if a gray quilt has been pulled across the sky. Thunder shakes the island and the coconut trees tremble in the wind. Cziczee isn't afraid of the storm, and she isn't ready to go home. She can see the lightning flash from the clouds, hitting one of the smaller islands. Cziczee wonders what lightning is made of, and she wonders if it has a Latin name as well. As she thinks about this, she feels the hairs on her arms begin to rise. Her skin feels as if it is alive, buzzing. Suddenly, there is a loud crack, but

Cziczee doesn't feel much more than a bristling, burning sensation, and hears a hollow ringing sound, a brassy echo in her ears.

Cziczee knows that she has been struck by lightning and she is no longer alive, but it doesn't frighten her. Instead, she feels an overwhelming sense of curiosity and relief, because all of the Latin words have been erased from her mind.

A few days later, she returns to the island as an arora. When her parents see her, they are overjoyed, even as their eyes fill with tears. She visits them each day, and though she cannot eat the food her mother makes or swim out to meet her father when he comes back from fishing, Cziczee continues to share in the housework and helps her father mend his nets. She also returns to see Professor Osgood, who squints at her in surprise and studies her with a magnifying glass. Cziczee no longer has to memorize Latin names, but she often slips into the professor's library, a musty room with shelves and shelves of books. Though she avoids everything written in Latin, she discovers plenty of other interesting books on science, history, and literature. A set of encyclopedias fills a shelf. Starting with *A*, she works her way to *Z*. Whenever Hezekiah Osgood enters the room, Cziczee quickly turns aside and disappears. Many of the books are difficult to read, but Cziczee finds a dictionary to help her understand the words. For the first time, she is studying useful things. She learns that lightning is a form of electricity and finds out that it actually moves upward from the earth rather than striking downward from the clouds. She learns all about electrons and positive and negative ions. As years go by, she reads almost all of the professor's books, except for a few dull volumes of philosophy that don't make any sense.

One day, while she is browsing through Osgood's library, Cziczee feels the hairs on her arms prickling. It's almost exactly the same feeling she had when she was struck by lightning. Not sure what is happening, Cziczee turns around to see Professor Osgood's camera aimed at her. Again there is a crackle and bang, a blinding flash of light, and a ringing sound in her inner ear, followed by silence. A short while later, she finds herself pressed against a blank sheet of paper. The professor takes out his magnifying glass and examines Cziczee carefully, as if she were a butterfly stuck on a pin. Soon afterward, he folds her into three sections, then stuffs her into an envelope and sends her off to France. Cziczee doesn't understand what is happening, but two months later she returns unopened, and the professor tucks the envelope inside a book.

23

O kay, but how do we get them out of these books?"

Ted Parker still didn't look convinced after his wife called him over to the library the next day and showed him the articles she had found with Orion and Ming's help.

"I don't know," said Alma. "Osgood doesn't say. But somehow he was able to glue these spirits onto the page and preserve their images."

As a chemistry teacher, Ted approached the arora with a scientist's skepticism. He held the book that Courtney had found up to the light and tilted it from side to side. Nalini's eyes followed him. He touched the apparition and felt nothing but the smooth texture of the paper. When he curled the paper gently, the ghost's image remained flush with the page. Turning off the light in Alma's office and drawing the shades, he noticed that the ghost emitted its own light, a dull phosphorescent glow that made it visible in the dark.

"I'm going to take this back to the lab at school and test it," he said. "Maybe I can find out what it's made of. I'd also like to look at the image under a microscope. I'm sure there's some rational explanation."

"Please don't do anything that would harm her," said Alma. "The poor woman looks as if she's suffered enough."

"Don't worry. I'll be careful," said Ted with a wink. "I know how to treat a library book."

A few minutes after Ted left, Courtney, Ming, and Orion came through the main entrance of the library. Once again, Courtney had been able to persuade her mother to let her come to the library, supposedly to do her homework. Alma gestured for the three of them to follow her into the office and closed the door.

"I still don't know if any of this is true or not," she said. "But no matter what, we've got a lot of work to do. I want you to go down to the stacks and find every book that contains a ghost and bring it to my office."

She handed them several sheets of paper.

"This is a list of all the books that were donated to the library from the estate of Hezekiah Osgood. Each of them will have the same bookplate."

"What are we going to do with the ghosts after we get them all together?" asked Courtney.

"I haven't figured that out," said Alma. "But it's important to make sure that nobody else checks out these books. I don't want to cause a panic. Luckily, only Marigold has spotted one, but if people think that the library is haunted, we'll have a lot more problems on our hands."

As they began to search the stacks, each with a different section of the list, Ming found the book from which the envelope had fallen yesterday. She was sure Ms. Parker would get angry with her for having taken it. But when she showed the letter to the librarian, along with the picture of the girl with pigtails, Ms. Parker was so preoccupied reading the letter, she didn't say anything.

Courtney had been assigned to the reference section, most of which was empty of ghosts, though she did find a couple of dazed-looking castaways in the *Encyclopedia of Modern Telepathy*. Meanwhile, Orion was searching the fiction shelves, surrounded by novels and collections of short stories. One of the books on his list was *Operation Johnny Rook*, about a secret agent who parachutes onto an iceberg. Orion wanted to keep reading but forced himself to flip ahead and see if there were any ghosts. On the last page of the book, he found an arora about his own age. The ghost was a scruffy boy with thick black hair that seemed to have been recently cut but never combed. He had a bored expression on his face, but his eyes brightened when he saw Orion, as if he might be looking to make friends. The arora had a pocketknife in one hand, and as Orion watched, the boy touched the tip of the blade to his chin, then flipped the knife downward with a casual gesture. Retrieving it from the ground, he repeated the action, pressing the knife to his ear, his forehead, and his nose, each in turn. Puzzled, Orion watched the arora for a while, then reluctantly closed the novel and moved on to find the next title on his list.

24

The game is called mumblety-peg, and the arora's name is Tarquin Tao-Jenkins. He learns how to play mumblety-peg after
he is kidnapped by pirates. The whole point of the game is to toss
a knife at the ground or onto the deck of a ship and make it stick
point first. You start by touching the knife to your chin, then flick
it away from yourself so it spins and lands on the sharp end of the
blade. After that you touch your nose, your forehead, your ear, etc.
Mumblety-peg takes skill and patience, but it's a good way to
pass the time, especially when you're held hostage for months
aboard a leaky pirate ship that's stuck in the doldrums.

Tarquin is an orphan, which is why nobody is willing to pay a
ransom for his release. The pirates who capture him in Macao realize too late that he has no family or benefactors of any kind. His father, an English soap merchant, is dead. His mother, a Chinese opera
singer, is also dead. Tarquin has no one to support him and lives on
his own, begging and occasionally stealing whatever he needs off the
streets of Macao. He doesn't really mind being kidnapped because

it is an adventure, and he makes friends with most of the pirates, except for one or two hard-boiled buccaneers who resent the fact that he hasn't brought them any ransom. They want to throw him overboard, but the others decide to keep Tarquin on as a deck hand.

From Macao, the pirates sail through the Malacca straits and wander around the Bay of Bengal in search of plunder, then drift southward, circumventing the tip of India, past Serendip, where they have a fierce gun battle with a British frigate. Their ship is already full of holes, and a cannonball punctures the hull just above the waterline so that they barely escape over the horizon. After weeks of no wind and seas as still and limpid as liquid jade, they finally catch the Bromiel current that pulls them toward Prithvideep.

When he isn't bailing out water or swabbing the decks, Tarquin spends most of his day playing mumblety-peg. Eventually, during a storm, the pirate ship crashes into a reef off the main island of Prithvideep. Everyone on board is killed, including Tarquin, who discovers that drowning isn't as bad as he thought it was going to be, a bit like gargling salt water, without being able to spit. Much to his surprise, he finds himself cast ashore as a ghost. This isn't exactly the escape he'd planned, but it's not unpleasant either. After the tragedy and struggle of being an orphan, and the whole pirate kidnapping episode, becoming an arora on Ilhas dos Fantasmas is a welcome change. Though Tarquin is a loner by nature, he gets to know some of the other spirits on the island and learns their language. The only reminder of his past life is the pocketknife that Tarquin still carries, which helps him pass the time as he plays endless games of mumblety-peg.

Eventually, after seventy-five years on the island, he's kidnapped again. This time, it isn't pirates who take him hostage but a weird old man with a rickety-looking contraption that fires like a cannon. There is so much smoke and sparks, Tarquin is sure he's been shot, but the next thing he knows he's a prisoner inside a book. He also knows that nobody is going to rescue him, except maybe the boy who finally opens the novel and stares at him with questioning eyes.

25

Even though it was a Friday afternoon and school was over for the day, Roberta Hokum was just starting to get busy. First, she went to Mr. Abernathy's office and insisted that the principal call the superintendent and each of the members of the school board to report the incident at the library. Then she drove across town to speak with Carville's chief of police, Morris Burpee. He was a large man in his mid-sixties who had been on the force for over thirty years. Chief Burpee had seen everything in the town from double-parked cars on Main Street to the bodies of murder victims floating in cranberry bogs.

"Are you sure it's serious?" he said. "These kids were probably just fooling around, and one of them got scared. It happens all the time, Mrs. Hokum."

"No, I spoke with Marigold's mother," said Roberta. "She kept her daughter home from school today because the poor child was so upset."

"But the girl's okay, isn't she?" said Chief Burpee.

"Yes, thank goodness, though she's been badly traumatized."

"Why didn't her mother call me herself?"

"Well, she isn't really sure what happened," said Roberta, trying to remain calm and polite. "Chief Burpee, there's definitely something wrong with that library. I've been saying it for years. The place is infested and dangerous. It's full of books that children shouldn't be exposed to—terrible stories with tragic endings, ugly descriptions of unpleasant places, biographies of criminals and thugs, scientific theories that haven't been proven, histories of countries that no longer exist. Why, it's an absolute disgrace that we should have this kind of library in our town!"

"Now let me get this straight," said Chief Burpee, leaning forward across his desk. "You want me to investigate the library because you don't like the books that it contains?"

"Exactly," said Roberta. "Our children face a terrible risk. We have to protect them from these corrupting influences."

"Sorry. There's nothing I can do," the police chief said, shaking his head. "If you've got a problem with those books, then speak to Alma Parker, the head librarian."

"But I have!" Roberta's voice was beginning to get shrill. "All she said was that she'd look into it. I know Alma Parker won't do anything at all. She's hiding something."

"Well, I'm afraid I can't help you. Unless there's some kind of danger, or a law has been broken, the police can't go into the library and take books off the shelves."

"But don't you see, there *is* a danger!" said Roberta. "Our children are being threatened. It's not just the books. That building is so old it should be condemned. The floors feel as if they're going to collapse, and the carpets are full of mold and fungus. If nothing else, it's possible that Marigold is suffering from an acute allergic reaction."

"In that case, Mrs. Hokum, you should speak to the building inspector," said Chief Burpee. "I'm sorry I can't be more helpful, but it's really not my job. You can always complain to the town selectmen, if you'd like."

Leaving the police station in frustration, Roberta Hokum got back in her car and drove straight to the library. She was determined to stop whatever was going on. By this time, it was almost five o'clock. As she pushed her way through the main door, Roberta didn't notice anything out of the ordinary. A few people were reading magazines; a woman with two young children was checking out books at the desk, where one of the assistant librarians was on duty. Someone was using the photocopying machine, which rattled and creaked. With purposeful strides, the sixth-grade teacher headed for the stacks.

As she started down the stairs, she met Orion coming up in the opposite direction. He was carrying a pile of books in his arms.

"What are you doing here?" she demanded.

Orion didn't know what to say at first.

"We're . . . we're helping Ms. Parker," he stammered.

Roberta snatched one of the books he was carrying and looked at the cover as if it were some kind of bomb.

" 'Weather Patterns in the Indian Ocean,' " she read. "Is this for your World's Fair report?"

"Maybe," said Orion, terrified that she was going to open the book. Mrs. Hokum's face looked like an angry mask. He watched as his teacher suspiciously turned the book over in her hands before giving it back.

"Where are you taking these?"

"To Ms. Parker's office."

"Is anyone else with you?"

Orion nodded.

Roberta Hokum's high heels clattered on the steps as she brushed past him and descended into the stacks.

Downstairs, Courtney and Ming were leafing through a book of nautical history to see if it contained a ghost. When Ming saw Mrs. Hokum, her first reaction was to close the book and quickly put it back on the shelf.

"Wait!" said Roberta. "Ming, I want to see that book. Give it to me this minute!"

The two girls looked at each other, afraid to move. By this time, Orion had already warned Alma Parker. She came rushing out of her office and down the stairs into the stacks. After that, everything seemed to happen at once, as if a tornado had struck.

As soon as Roberta Hokum saw the librarian, she glanced about her and found a fire alarm on the wall. Reaching over, she grabbed the red handle and yanked it down. The alarm immediately went off with a sharp ringing sound, amplified by the basement walls and low ceiling. The bell was so loud it drowned out the confused clamor of their voices along with shouts and cries of panic as everyone rushed out of the library. A few minutes later, they could hear sirens coming up the road from the fire station.

26

As the nurse trundled the cart full of medicine bottles, thermometers, and syringes down the hallway, she was humming to herself. The building was quiet and still, as if all of the residents were asleep. The wheels on the cart rolled softly over the plush green carpet. Between each of the doors were pictures on the walls, cheerful prints of famous paintings by artists like Rousseau and Gauguin. It made the long hallway feel like a museum.

Knocking at Room 28, the nurse listened for a moment, but there was no reply. She turned the knob and pushed the cart inside.

"Good evening, Nick. Time to take your pills."

No answer came from the figure in the wheelchair, who was facing the window. His head was slumped to one side, and his left hand was draped over the armrest.

The nurse quickly checked the old man's breathing and then his pulse. She put her fingers on his wrist and then she touched his neck but found no sign of life. Nick Osgood's eyes were closed, and there was a wistful smile on his colorless lips, a look of contentment. The tattoo on the old man's cheek was like a blue inkspot on his pale white skin. He seemed to have passed away peacefully, without the slightest struggle. The only sign of disruption was the broken thumb piano on the floor. It had fallen from Nick's hands and shattered. The carved coconut shell had broken into a dozen fragments, and the metal tines were strewn about like petals of steel.

27

Courtney, Ming, and Orion were standing outside the library as the fire trucks pulled into the parking lot with their sirens wailing and lights flashing. Alma Parker was speaking with a policeman, who had been the first to arrive. Mrs. Hokum stood by herself with her arms crossed and a serene look of satisfaction on her face. The alarm inside the library was still ringing, a persistent shriek that made it seem as if the building itself were possessed by a tortured spirit.

Firemen in yellow coats and rubber boots jumped out of the trucks and rushed inside, carrying axes. For a few minutes, it felt as if there really were a fire, but finally the alarm was switched off. By now the policeman was talking to Mrs. Hokum, who was waving her arms and pointing at the library, as if she could actually see flames.

Ms. Parker came over to where Orion, Ming, and Courtney were standing. She shook her head in dismay.

"Thanks for all your help, but I think you should go home

now," she said. "We won't be able to do anything more today. We can finish up tomorrow. I'll be here at eight in the morning. It's Saturday, so the library doesn't open until noon. That should give us enough time to get most of the books off the shelves."

As they unlocked their bicycles and started home, Courtney led the way. Instead of turning left on Elm Street, as they usually did, she wheeled to the right.

"Where are you going?" shouted Ming.

"Come on," said Courtney, "I want to show you something."

"What is it?" said Orion, pedaling hard to catch up.

"You'll see."

By now the sun was starting to go down, though there was still another hour until it would get dark. As Courtney and the others coasted down the hill, they could see the harbor in front of them, the marina full of sailboats and the lighthouse in the distance. It was a clear spring evening, with a promise of summer in the air. Halfway down the hill, Courtney signaled to turn left, and Ming realized they were heading into the cemetery.

"Why are we here?" she asked when they stopped.

"I found something yesterday," said Courtney, "on my way home from school."

"More ghosts?" said Orion.

"No. You'll see. We have to leave our bikes outside the gate."

The cemetery was spread over the slope of the hill overlooking Hornswoggle Bay. Many of those who were buried here had been sailors and fishermen. The trees in the cemetery were mostly oaks and maples and a huge horse chestnut with leafy branches that sheltered the stones beneath. Just inside the gate was a memorial for soldiers and sailors killed during the First and Second World Wars. There was also a memorial for fishermen lost at sea, a circular stone carved in the shape of a ship's wheel. In the center was the emblem of an anchor and a codfish. Names and dates were carved below. Ming noticed that the most recent deaths had been recorded only a year ago. She remembered reading how a fishing trawler had disappeared during a storm, and the crew was never found.

Courtney guided them past a line of old slate markers on which the names and dates were barely visible. Though the cemetery was carefully maintained and the grass was neatly cut, the ancient tombstones leaned this way and that, like dominoes about to fall. On ahead they passed more recent graves, some with simple memorials, others with elaborately carved images of angels and crosses. The granite markers had all been quarried from the sea rocks at Headstone Point. There were flowers and flags in front of some of the stones. Shrubs grew along the pathways that twisted and turned like a maze. Sections of the graveyard were terraced, and as the friends climbed the hill, they came to a staircase, partly covered with moss, leading up to one of the largest tombs. The mausoleum was about six feet high and made of granite, parts of which were roughly finished, contrasting with the domed roof and polished pillars in front. Amidst all of the other graves, this monument looked out of place, like a Greek or Egyptian temple that had been closed up for centuries. Framed between the pillars was a marble plaque.

OSGOOD
Clara Murchison Osgood
1883–1951
Devoted Wife of
Hezekiah Tiberius Osgood
1880–1983

"And look at that." Courtney pointed to the triangular lintel above the pillars. In the center was the carved shape of a conch shell with wings.

"Hezekiah Osgood must have built this for his wife. His body is buried here as well," said Courtney.

"Is anything else written on the tomb?" asked Orion.

They circled the granite crypt but found nothing. There were no openings or windows. The whole tomb looked so solid and sealed, it gave Courtney a feeling of claustrophobia, even though she was standing outside. Ming glanced at her watch.

"It's almost five thirty. I need to get home," she said. Turning, she caught her breath. Without a word, Ming reached out and grabbed Courtney's arm. Nothing had really changed, but everything was suddenly different.

"What is it?" Courtney asked.

"I thought I saw something," said Ming.

"Where?" said Orion.

"Right here. Someone was standing beside that pillar."

The three of them remained absolutely still. Sunlight was filtering through the trees, and the distant waves on the ocean looked like rumpled silk. A couple of seagulls were circling overhead. There was nothing to be frightened about, yet it felt as if an invisible shadow had fallen over the tomb. They could feel an unknown presence, like the delicate wings of a moth brushing against their skin.

"There he is!"

This time Orion was the first to see the figure, an old man, about six feet tall, with stooped shoulders. Though his hair and eyebrows were completely white and his skin had no color at all, an amber tint surrounded his image, a sepia aura. The ghost looked as if he had just jumped out of a tree and landed in front of them. For a man of his age, his eyes were young, full of childish curiosity. Ming could feel her knees knocking, and Orion wanted to run, though his feet seemed glued to the ground. Even Courtney got ready to scream. Seeing ghosts inside a book or a letter was one thing, but standing face-to-face with one was a completely different matter.

Standing beside the Osgoods' tomb, the spirit examined Courtney, Ming, and Orion with a bemused expression on his face. They dared not speak, and he said nothing. After his gray eyes had taken them in for several minutes, the figure turned, as if to walk away, and suddenly vanished.

Nobody moved.

"Do you think he'll come back?" said Courtney after a minute had passed.

"It must be Hezekiah's ghost," whispered Ming.

"I'm getting out of here," said Orion.

"Me too!"

They began to descend the mossy staircase, looking around them, as if they were being stalked. Halfway down the steps, Ming started to run, and the other two followed in a panic.

28

When Alma got home from the library, there was a message on her answering machine from Dr. Goldfarb. The doctor apologized for passing on sad news, but he said that Nick Osgood had died peacefully. Since there were no family members to be informed, and Alma was the last visitor, Dr. Goldfarb thought she might like to know. He said the Enoch Knox Funeral Home was handling all of the arrangements.

Alma sat down on the sofa to collect herself. The fire alarm at the library had been traumatic enough, and now this news. She had never really known Nick Osgood but recalled the excitement in his eyes when she first opened the book for him and he saw the arora. She remembered the way he'd spoken to the image, the enthusiasm in his voice, even though the words were unintelligible. More than anything, she had hoped that Nick could help her communicate with the phantoms, but that wasn't possible anymore. The only living link to the spirits of Prithvideep was gone, and the librarian felt helpless and afraid.

Moments later, Alma heard the front door open, and her husband came in, holding the library book in his hand. Before Alma could tell Ted what had happened, he said, "There's nothing here. I've done everything I can to test the image, but it doesn't exist. When I put it under a microscope, all I could see were the magnified letters and paper. When I did a litmus test, the strip didn't turn pink or blue. I tried using magnets and ultraviolet light. I tested it for radiation. I scanned it for any trace of chemicals. I even checked for bacteria and mold, but there's no scientific evidence that anything is inside this book. It doesn't make sense. You can see the image, but there's absolutely nothing there."

"Nick Osgood passed away," said Alma.

Ted looked at her blankly for a moment.

"When?" he said.

"This afternoon. I think we should go to the funeral home to pay our respects. The poor man didn't have any family. He was so old that all of his friends must be dead. I feel somehow responsible. Will you come with me?"

"Now?"

"It's only seven o'clock. Come on, Ted, we'll get some flowers along the way."

By the time they reached the funeral home, it was dark, and lights were glowing in all the windows. The widow's watch, with its conical roof, looked like a forbidden tower. Alma could imagine the professor locked away up there with his experiments.

When they rang the bell, the sound echoed from somewhere deep inside the house. Alma held a bouquet of red carnations in a vase that she had bought at the florist. For a couple of minutes there was no response, until they heard the shuffling of footsteps on the stairs and the rattle of keys. The brass knob twisted back and forth, as if it were stuck, before the door finally opened to let them in. Alma recognized Enoch Knox, who was a familiar figure in the town. His dark suit fit him with snug confinement, as if it had been sewed onto his bulky frame. His moustache drooped, and his eyes were small and sad. He spoke with a lisp.

"Good evening. May I help you?"

"We heard about Nick Osgood's death. I understand you're handling the funeral arrangements."

"Ah, yes . . . the dearly departed."

"I'm sorry, we didn't mean to come so late, but we only just found out."

"Are you related to the deceased?"

"No, just friends. Acquaintances. . . . I'm Alma Parker, from the library."

"Yes, of course."

"We could come back tomorrow, if it's not convenient," said Ted.

"No. No. No inconvenience at all. If you'll step this way into the viewing parlor. . . ."

Though all of the lamps in the funeral home were on, none of them were very bright, and the rooms were dim, as if the wallpaper absorbed most of the light. Following Enoch Knox into the parlor, Alma could see the open casket, and she took her husband's arm. The body was dressed in a suit, exactly like the one the mortician wore. Nick Osgood's face was drawn but peaceful, and his hands were folded across his chest. The long fingers were thin and white like twigs of driftwood. Alma remembered how they had moved over the keys on the thumb piano. Now they were perfectly still.

She placed the vase of carnations on the table beside the coffin and looked at the old man's face, which had been powdered and made up. It seemed like a mask.

"When is the funeral?" she asked.

Enoch Knox leaned toward them and whispered confidentially, as if he were afraid of waking the dead.

"A somewhat unusual request," he said. "But we must honor the wishes of the deceased. According to his last will and testament, he asked for a burial at sea. We are making the arrangements and hope to complete everything by tomorrow afternoon. Will you be able to attend?"

"We'll try to be there," said Alma. "What time?"

"Four o'clock. At the fishing dock in the harbor."

Alma kept looking at Nick Osgood's features. His fine, white hair was perfectly combed, and his lips were pressed together in a lifeless smile. The lids of his eyes were closed but seemed almost translucent. For another five minutes they stood silently beside the casket, then took their leave. As they stepped out into the foyer, Alma looked up at the stained glass window at the top of the stairs. Though it was dark outside, she could still make out the design of the conch shell with wings.

"This house belonged to Nick's parents, didn't it?" said Alma, as Enoch Knox showed them to the door.

"Yes, I believe it did," said the mortician. "My late uncle, may he rest in peace, bought it after Professor Osgood died."

"Have you ever noticed anything strange about the house?" said Alma. "Anything mysterious or unexplained?"

Ted glared at her and tried to guide her outside, but Alma let go of his arm.

"Strange?" said Knox, confused. "Mysterious? Unexplained?"

"You know," said Alma, "some sort of phenomenon that doesn't make sense."

The mortician's eyes grew smaller and sadder. He ran the back of his hand across his drooping moustache.

"Do you mean ghosts?" he said.

"Yes," said Alma. "Well, not exactly. But something like that. Is this house haunted?"

By now, Ted was already halfway through the door, and he reached out to pull his wife after him.

"Haunted . . . ?" said Enoch Knox, his voice trailing off with a regretful sigh. "No. I'm afraid we have no ghosts."

29

Ming woke up to hear a tapping. She had been in the middle of a frustrating dream, standing at the front of a classroom while trying to give an oral report. Everyone was staring at her, including Mrs. Hokum, but Ming couldn't remember what she wanted to say. The papers she held were blank, and they kept slipping out of her fingers and onto the floor. Someone was laughing—it was Marigold Deitz. Mrs. Hokum was drumming her pencil impatiently on her desk, and the teacher's face gradually began to change, the lipstick smile turning into a toothless scowl, the pearl earrings transformed into rusty fishhooks, and her mascara congealing into a crusted scab. . . .

That was when Ming sat up in bed. For a moment, she couldn't figure out the sound that woke her. It was the same as Mrs. Hokum's pencil tapping on the desk. Then she realized it was coming from the window.

Nervously, she got out of bed and went across to see who it was, still picturing the horrible face from her dream. Peering through the glass, she saw Courtney standing outside and quietly slid the window open.

"What is it?"

"Come on. Get dressed."

The faint glow of the streetlight on the corner cast a yellow sheen through the maples in Ming's yard. Orion was standing a few feet behind Courtney, hands stuffed in both pockets.

"What time is it?" whispered Ming.

"One o'clock. Hurry."

Pulling on her jeans and a shirt in the dark, Ming searched for her socks and shoes. She brushed down her hair with both hands and tried to rub the sleep out of her eyes. Climbing through the window, she dropped to the ground.

"Where are we going this time?"

"I don't know," said Courtney, under her breath.

"What do you mean?"

"He wants to take us somewhere."

Ming glanced at Orion, but he looked as puzzled as she was.

"Who's taking us?" she said.

"Him," said Courtney, pointing to her left.

Ming turned around and saw the old man from the cemetery. He was standing at the edge of the driveway. In the dark, his features were less distinct, but it looked as if a pale light were shining through him. As Ming stared at the ghost in disbelief, he raised his hand and waved impatiently, then pointed down the street. It was obvious he wanted them to follow him, but when he turned he disappeared.

"Let's go," said Courtney.

Orion looked at Ming and rolled his eyes. The three of them started walking quickly in the direction the old man had gestured. Her voice lowered, Courtney explained that the spirit had come to her house and awakened her.

"I can't understand a word he's saying, but I know he needs our help."

"This is crazy," said Orion.

"Well, you didn't have to come," said Courtney. "Go back home if you want."

"Yeah, and spend the rest of the night awake, wondering what's going on?"

When they reached the end of the street, the ghost was waiting for them. Though he was an old man, he was able to move much more quickly than they, racing ahead. This time he directed them to turn right, past a gas station on the corner. Though it was closed, the lights were on and the three of them crossed over to the shadows on the other sidewalk. The ghost led them through the town until they came to the corner of Harbor Road and Longfellow Street. Most of the lights in the funeral home had been turned off, except for two lamps on the ground floor that glimmered like a pair of attentive eyes.

Enoch Knox had gone home just before midnight, closing Nick Osgood's casket and locking up the funeral home. But the ghost had entered through a crack in the door. He was now standing at the window, staring out at the three friends.

"Are you kidding? He wants us to go in there?" said Orion. "That's insane. I bet there are dead bodies in the basement."

"It must be important," said Courtney.

"Breaking into a library is one thing," said Ming. "But a funeral home . . ."

"We aren't breaking in. Look—he's opened the window for us."

"That still doesn't make it all right."

"I'm sure this has something to do with the books. If we don't go inside, we'll never find out."

Tiptoeing across the lawn, the three of them made their way to the window. One after the other, they scrambled inside. The dim lamps with velvet shades cast shallow pools of light on the carpeted floor, but beyond this was darkness. It took a moment for their eyes to adjust, then Ming nudged Orion. At the far end of the room lay a coffin with a vase of carnations by its side. The ghost had vanished, then reappeared beside the casket. Courtney was the only one who stepped forward when he beckoned.

"I bet it's empty," said Ming.

"I don't want to find out," Orion whispered as the phantom gently lifted the lid.

Courtney was close enough to see the body—the dark suit and folded hands. But it was the face that made her freeze. The ghost looked at her, and she could see immediately that it was the same person in the casket. They had identical features and thin white hair. One face was like a mask of the other. By this time, Orion and Ming had retreated a couple of steps toward the window, but just as they were about to escape, the ghost began to speak. It was a low mumble, like someone whispering through a keyhole. Yet his voice was persuasive and reassuring, even if the words didn't make any sense.

The spirit glanced at the corpse for a few seconds, as if he were observing his reflection in a mirror, before he lowered the lid of the casket. Then he slipped away from the coffin, moving toward an arched doorway that opened into the hall. None of the three friends moved until they heard his voice calling. When they saw him next, he was standing beside the banister of the staircase that led to the second floor.

"Did you bring your flashlight?" Courtney asked Orion.

"Of course," he said, biting his lip.

"I hope you've got new batteries this time," said Ming.

Taking the flashlight out of his pocket, Orion switched it on. The ghost seemed to be able to move through the dark without any trouble, but the yellow beam lit up the stairs as the three friends made their way to the top. Most of the rooms on the upper floor were empty, except for cardboard boxes and a few pieces of furniture and equipment. One was a machine with tubes and pumps that made Orion cringe as he imagined what purpose it served. The ghost had vanished again. While they waited for him to reappear, they peered about nervously. It smelled like mothballs and embalming fluid, a chemical sweetness. Suddenly there was the sound of a door being unlatched, followed by a creaking of un-oiled hinges that made them jump.

Orion turned his flashlight toward the sound, and they saw the ghost standing at the foot of another staircase leading up to the widow's watch. These steps were much steeper and narrower, twisting in a spiral. At the top lay a small circular room, barely large enough to hold them all. Ming felt uncomfortable standing so close to the ghost. As the phantom raised his hand toward the ceiling, his elbow bumped against Ming, but when she squeezed past him it felt as if nobody were there. A single window, with small diamond-shaped panes of glass, looked out over the harbor. The lighthouse was visible in the distance, its beacon shining like a fallen star.

The ghost was struggling with something on the ceiling, his thin, bony hands clawing at the textured surface. When Orion pointed the flashlight above them, it shone through the old man's arm, though the color of the beam changed from an electric yellow to cloudy white. Some of the plaster on the ceiling broke loose, and they could see the corner of a trapdoor. The old man was now able to work his fingers underneath and tugged on the door until it broke free.

The three of them looked up at the vacant black square overhead. Cautiously, Orion shone his flashlight inside, but there was nothing to see, as if the secret door opened onto a starless sky. Once again the ghost had vanished.

"How are we going to get up there without a ladder?" said Courtney.

"Why would anyone want to go up there?" said Orion.

"Because he opened it for us," Courtney answered.

"Yes, and now he's gone, which isn't very helpful." Orion brushed bits of plaster off his shirt.

"I'm sure he'll be back in a minute. Maybe if you and I lift Ming on our shoulders, she can crawl inside."

"No, thanks," said Ming. "Orion's the one with the flashlight. We can lift him up. It's not that high."

They waited a couple more minutes, but there was no sign of the ghost.

"Maybe he's gone," said Orion. "Maybe this is a portal to another world, and he's escaped."

"I don't think so. Why would he need us?" said Ming.

"Come on, Orion. We'll lift you up," said Courtney.

He looked at them with a reluctant frown, then nodded as Courtney made a cradle with her hands to hold one foot. Stepping up, Orion reached for the edge of the trapdoor. As he was lifted off the ground, Ming grabbed his other foot and hoisted him higher. They looked like a trio of clumsy acrobats. For a moment, Orion was sure he was going to fall, but finally they caught their balance, and he was able to wedge himself through the door and up onto his elbows. The air inside the attic was cooler and smelled like decaying wood. Twisting around, Orion reached for the flashlight in his pocket, but before he could switch it on, he saw the ghost kneeling a few feet away. The old man was holding something in his hands. It was impossible to see what it was in the dark. The flashlight revealed the conical shape of the roof and rafters converging overhead. The ghost looked at Orion and nodded, then held out the object he was holding—a human skull.

Orion would have jumped down, except that Courtney and Ming were holding his feet, and his elbows were wedged in place so that he couldn't move. The ghost seemed to want him to take the skull, but Orion's free hand was clenched into a fist. In the other hand the flashlight was shaking badly. He could feel himself breaking out in a cold sweat. At the same time, there was a reassuring look in the spirit's eyes, as if there were nothing wrong with holding a human skull. Orion began to feel he had no choice. His fingers slowly unknotted, and he finally took the skull in his free hand. It was lighter than he expected, like an empty cereal bowl. The eye sockets and nose, as well as the jaws and teeth, were intact, but the upper dome of the skull had been cut away, like a melon sliced in half.

"Are you okay?" Courtney called up to him.

"Yeah. S-sort of . . . ," Orion stuttered "You can let me down. Slowly."

Ming and Courtney began to lower him as carefully as they could. More plaster began to fall as his arms scraped against the sides of the trapdoor. The two girls dropped him awkwardly to the floor, while Orion tried not to lose his grip on the flashlight or the skull.

"What's that?" asked Courtney.

"What does it look like?" said Orion.

"I know it's a skull, but why is the top cut off?" said Courtney.

"There's something inside," said Ming.

"It looks like a giant fork or a comb," said Courtney.

"With metal fingers," Orion added.

"Like a miniature xylophone," said Ming.

30

It's a thumb piano."

Alma Parker picked up the gruesome instrument from her desk. She cautiously plucked at one of the metal tines attached to a bridge of whalebone inside the skull. The sound it made was not very loud, a single note like the solitary chime of an antique clock striking the hour. She pressed another key, and this time the note was higher pitched, the vibrations amplified by the hollow cranium.

"Where did you get this?" she asked.

Orion, Ming, and Courtney looked at one another, none of them wanting to answer the question. Finally, Ming spoke up and explained what had happened the night before.

"Where is this ghost?" Alma asked.

"We don't know. He disappeared as soon as we left the funeral home," said Courtney.

"That house used to belong to Hezekiah Osgood," Alma explained. "He must have brought this thumb piano with him from

Ilhas dos Fantasmas. It's mentioned in his book. This is one of the instruments that was used by necromancers to summon the arora."

"Maybe it can help us get them out of the books," said Orion.

"That's possible," said Alma. "But I think it's much more complicated. From what I've read so far, Professor Osgood used some kind of camera to trap the ghosts. He took their photographs, and in the process he was able to capture their images. He glued the arora inside these books and hid them away for all these years."

"Let's try it," said Courtney, taking one of the books from the librarian's desk. Opening it, she found the image of a young child, three or four years old. He looked up at them from the page, as if he had just woken out of a nap and was about to cry.

Orion picked up the skull and, holding it in both hands, positioned his thumbs over the keys. The first few notes he struck were barely audible. Even so, tears formed in the child's eyes, and his lower lip began to tremble. Orion plucked the keys a little harder, and the sound came out much louder and clearer. It almost felt as if the instrument were playing itself, his thumbs moving faster now, back and forth across the flexible tines—up and down the scale. In many ways, the thumb piano wasn't that different from the controller of a video game, except that there were metal keys instead of buttons, and rather than holding a plastic console in his hands, Orion's fingers were wrapped around a human skull. The music that came from the thumb piano was less of a tune or melody and more like the sound of tiny coins falling into a copper bowl.

The child in the book was smiling now, listening to the thumb piano. He lifted a hand, as if to reach out and touch the music, but his image was still fixed to the page. As Orion kept playing, the child nodded drowsily in time to the beat, and his mouth opened in a happy yawn.

"He can hear you, but it doesn't seem to have any other effect," said Courtney. "Maybe there's some special kind of music to break the spell."

By this time Orion had figured out how to play "Twinkle Twinkle Little Star," picking at the keys one by one.

"That's definitely not going to work," said Ming as he hit a wrong note.

"Look!" said Ms. Parker, her voice catching in her throat.

All three of them turned and saw the old man's ghost leaning against the wall. He was staring intently at Orion, who continued playing the thumb piano. By now the child had fallen asleep, and Courtney gently closed the covers of the book, as if she were tucking the ghost into bed.

"Hello, Nick," said Alma, after taking a deep breath.

31

The ghost nods in recognition. Though he stands in front of them and is conscious of his surroundings—the desk piled high with old books, the coffeemaker gurgling in one corner, the framed photograph of Ted Parker on Alma's desk, and the thumb piano in Orion's hands—Nick feels a strange detachment from the scene. Entering the room is like stepping through a melting pane of glass into a fluid world. Everything is familiar, but the perspective has changed, as if all of the angles are skewed and the air itself is warped. Having been a ghost for less than twenty-four hours, Nick is still getting used to the experience. The hardest part is keeping his balance, and he feels a sense of vertigo, as if everything were tipping side to side. It is like being in a fishing boat on a rough sea, except that these are waves of light and sound instead of water. There is no strong force of gravity, only the pull of his own volition, so that the slightest movement carries him much farther and faster than if he were alive.

"Can you hear me? Can you tell us what's going on?"

Now he knows the woman's voice. She is the one who visited him in the nursing home.

"We need your help, Nick," she says. "Why did you want us to have this thumb piano?"

He knows the answer but cannot form the words.

"Why are these ghosts inside the books?" she continues.

Toward the end of his life, Nick had felt his memory fading. In the nursing home, all he could remember were fragments from childhood, happy memories of playing on a beach, collecting seashells, games with other children, chasing each other around the columns of coconut trees. He had lost all sense of time, except for moments plucked from the keys on his thumb piano, the soothing tempo of those notes. But now he has regained his lost memories. It all comes pouring back, as if a curtain has been drawn aside and sunlight is streaming through a window. He knows that he is dead, yet he is able to reclaim the erased memories of his life—the fishing boat and the store near the harbor, Nick's Bait and Tackle, the company of old friends who gather in the evenings and swap stories.

"Can you tell us what your father did?"

The woman's question interrupts his reverie.

"How did Professor Osgood get these images into the books? Is there any way to take them out? Please, Nick, we need your help. Try to remember."

Yes, he knows the truth, or part of it—how his father captures the arora with his camera, stealing their light. Nick can never forgive Hezekiah for destroying his idyllic childhood and for the tragedy and suffering he causes. But until now, Nick doesn't realize where the ghosts are hidden, secretly tucked between the pages of his father's books. If only he knew this earlier, Nick might have been able to rescue his friends.

"What is it, Nick? Tell us?"

He stares down at the books and reaches out a hand to touch them, feeling the texture of the covers. Lifting a volume, he weighs it in his hand, as if to measure the consequences. Nick understands what has to be done. Opening the book, he sees the familiar face that looks back at him. It is Porquoix, his childhood friend, one of Nick's closest companions. Even though Porquoix is an arora, they played together on the island. Porquoix remains a boy, while Nick is now a frail old man. Yet they still recognize each other as friends.

"Don't worry, Porquoix," says Nick under his breath. "I'll set you free."

"What are you saying?" the woman asks.

Nick slowly closes the book and stares at her.

"This should never have happened," he says, still speaking the language of the arora. "My father was an arrogant man, a scholar who looked down on everyone else. He went to Prithvideep to study primitive people—to elucidate their culture—but in the end he turned out to be the greatest savage of us all. He was a heartless man whose books were nothing but bricks he used to build a prison wall. Professor Hezekiah Tiberius Osgood. Sounds impressive, doesn't it? Well, he didn't deserve that name. Hezekiah was a prophet. Tiberius an emperor. Great men. My father was not. He was a thief, a grave robber, but not like those who loot precious relics from a tomb. Instead, he stole the dead themselves. He pillaged their souls."

* * *

Alma and the others exchanged glances, puzzled by Nick's words. It wasn't a language they understood.

"Wait, there's a glossary in *The Compleat Necromancer*!" said Ming. "Maybe that will help."

Alma reached for the heavy green book and searched the pages until she came to a list of words and definitions.

"Speak slowly, Nick," said Alma.

"Koob dekciw a si taht," the ghost replied.

All four of them leaned over one another to try to find the definitions, but none of the words seemed to be in the glossary.

"Em ot netsil," Nick said impatiently. *"Srettel eht esrever!"*

"This isn't going to work," said Ming.

"I wish he'd say one word at a time," Orion complained.

"Arora," said Nick, pointing to himself.

"Hold on," said Courtney. "I know! *Arora* is a palindrome. It's spelled the same in both directions. That's why it's the only word we can understand. He's speaking *backwards*."

"That must be it," said Alma excitedly. "Write down what he says and we'll reverse the letters."

"Ti tog ev'uoy won," said Nick.

TEE TOG EVOY ONE

Ming copied down the sounds, then wrote them backward.

ENO YOVE GOT EET

"That still doesn't make sense."

In frustration, Nick reached out his hand and took Ming's pencil in his pale fingers. The letters he wrote were shaky but clear enough to read. He handed the pencil back and Ming rewrote the words:

NOW YOU'VE GOT IT

All of them looked up at the ghost, who nodded with satisfaction. Taking the pencil back he wrote:

AREMAC A DEEN EW

But as he was spelling the words there was a commotion outside, the sound of angry voices shouting and loud applause. Immediately, Nick disappeared and Orion, who was closest to the window, looked out into the parking lot of the library. A crowd of more than thirty people had gathered on the front steps, holding posters and banners.

SAVE OUR LIBRARY!
GOOD BOOKS, NOT EVIL!
WE WANT HAPPY ENDINGS!

Standing on the top step was Roberta Hokum, waving her hands like an orchestra conductor and leading the chants. Orion could see Marigold Deitz and her mother in the crowd, as well as more than a dozen parents and kids. Some of them were raising their fists in the air and others were linking their arms together in a chain of protest.

When Alma saw what was going on, she quickly took the thumb piano and hid it away in a locked drawer of her desk.

"All three of you stay inside," she said. "I'll deal with this."

"Be careful," said Orion. "Mrs. Hokum is crazy."

"Maybe we should call the police," said Ming.

"It's too late for that," said Courtney as Ms. Parker opened the front door of the library. The chanting grew louder and the protestors rushed forward. Before Alma could say anything, Roberta Hokum led the charge, pushing past her with Marigold and her mother following close behind. The rest of the crowd stayed on the steps, brandishing their posters and shouting in confusion, as Alma tried to block the entrance.

Inside the librarian's office, Ming, Orion, and Courtney braced themselves. Mrs. Hokum burst through the door and pointed a finger.

"Where is that book?"

Marigold stood by her teacher's side, smirking.

"Which book?" said Ming.

"You know what I'm talking about," said Mrs. Hokum.

"There it is!" Marigold pointed at the pile on the desk. "It's the bird book. With the yellow cover."

Before anyone else could react, Mrs. Hokum swooped forward and snatched it off the desk. She raised the book triumphantly above her head and went outside again. The protesters began to cheer.

"We've got it!" screamed Mrs. Hokum. "We've got it! This is the book!"

An eager hush fell over the crowd.

"Be careful, Roberta!" said Alma calmly, finally able to make herself heard. "It's not what you think!"

The teacher looked back at her with a scornful smile. She didn't even bother to open the book, holding it away from herself as if it were poisoned.

"Don't tell me to be careful!" she said. "We know what you're up to, Alma Parker. There's only one thing to do with a book like this."

Mrs. Hokum took a bottle of perfume out of her purse and poured it onto the book, dousing it completely. Then the teacher gestured to one of the parents in the crowd who handed her a cigarette lighter.

Flicking the lighter, Mrs. Hokum held the flame under the book, which began to smolder and smoke as the perfume ignited.

"No!" shouted Alma, rushing forward, but two of the protestors held her back. The book was soon burning like a torch, and Mrs. Hokum stood there holding it above her head like a demonic Statue of Liberty in high heels.

By this time, Ming had called 911. When the Carville police arrived, they dispersed the demonstrators. Roberta Hokum was led away by Chief Burpee, who threatened to arrest her for destroying public property. She continued to shout and scream, pointing an accusing finger at the library as she was bundled into the police car.

After she and the others were gone, Alma picked up the burned remains of the book, which lay on the front steps of the library, where Roberta had dropped it. The upper half of the book was badly charred and crumbled into ashes as soon as Alma touched it. The yellow cover was scorched, and the embossed image of the albatross was a blackened scar. Orion, Ming, and Courtney watched as the librarian opened the ruined volume. The colored plates of different species of birds had been burned around the edges, and the binding had warped. There was a bitter, smoky odor, mixed with the sickly stench of Mrs. Hokum's perfume. Almost afraid to look, Alma turned the disintegrating pages one by one, though she knew the ghost was no longer there. The fire had destroyed whatever spectral image the book contained—a "final death," as Professor

Osgood had described it. Even though the ghost had been a frightening spirit, with malevolent eyes and fishhooks in his ears, Alma felt as if a tragedy had occurred, a violation. The front cover of the book came loose in the librarian's hands, along with the first few pages. She saw the bookplate with the inkstand and the palm trees, as well as the emblem of the conch shell with wings. The corners had curled up from the heat, like the edges of a dying leaf.

There was nothing to do but take the book inside and get back to work. All four of them returned to Alma's office and silently began sorting the volumes into separate piles. Those that contained ghosts were put in a cabinet that could be locked, while the rest were set aside for re-shelving. After what had just happened they felt an added sense of urgency and determination.

32

Once again, darkness closes in around Porquoix. He listens for the music of the thumb piano, but the compressed layers of paper muffle all sounds. In desperation, Porquoix tries to call out his friend's name, but he knows it is useless.

"Nick! Nick! Where are you? Where have you gone?"

With Nick's face still clear in his mind's eye, Porquoix is overcome with excitement and nostalgia, recalling their childhood together. Though the years of darkness are difficult to measure, his earlier memories are as sharp and clear as mica glistening in the sand.

Porquoix remembers how the two of them first meet, soon after he becomes an arora. Nick is sitting by himself on the beach, skipping stones across the surface of the lagoon. He is bored and lonely, an only child with no companions, brought to this strange place by his parents. The other children on the island do not speak this boy's language, and he feels like a castaway. Porquoix approaches the boy, and the two of them stare at each other, in silence. When they speak, neither can understand the other, but it doesn't seem to matter. Over the first few days, Porquoix leads Nick around the island and shows him secrets that he discovered when he was still alive—a wild citrus tree that bears the sweetest fruit, the nest of an antipodean tern that contains the hatched shells of blue eggs, the mouth of a cave fringed with ferns. Together they creep inside, feeling the cool air blowing from deep inside the earth. The passage is narrow and dark. Nick follows Porquoix until they reach a hidden grotto where the tide flows in through a submerged channel in the reef. Crevices in the rocks overhead filter shafts of sunlight into this secret vault. Within the tidal pools, Nick discovers starfish that glow in the dark and mottled shells of different colors. The grotto becomes their hideaway, and the two boys—one alive, the other a ghost—spend hours together inside the cave. Porquoix teaches Nick his language, word by word, and soon they can speak together like brothers, sharing their dreams and fears.

Over time, the two friends grow so close that Porquoix seldom thinks of Nick as being any different from himself. Yet they are separated by the invisible curtains of the afterlife. Porquoix can grab Nick's arm or push him playfully into the sand, but his friend is unable to touch his companion in return. Sometimes Nick tries, forgetting their differences and reaching out to nudge Porquoix or trying to trip him up as they race each other along the beach. But there is nothing there, only the phantom image, through which his fingers pass as if waving at smoke.

A week or two after they meet, Porquoix leads Nick to the bungalow where he lived when he was alive. His mother is still there, wearing her blue pinafore. She greets her lost son with a smile and shakes hands with his friend. Together they go inside the house and into Porquoix's room, which is just as he left it on the day he was killed by the shark. On a shelf above his bed, Nick notices a carved coconut shell and, taking it down, he discovers it is a thumb piano. While the arora stands by attentively, Nick plucks at the keys, and the notes ring out. He looks at Porquoix and sees that the ghost is smiling. For the first time he feels as if he can touch his friend, as if the music travels from his fingers through the keys and into the empty air. Waves of sound connect them like delicate filaments that run from one life to the next. After that, whenever Nick wants to call his friend, he plays a few notes on the thumb piano, and Porquoix appears.

One day, Nick points to the tattoo on his friend's cheek and asks him what it is.

"A sign," Porquoix tells him, "a symbol of these islands."

"But what does it mean?" asks the boy.

"There's an old story, a folktale. They say that when a person dies, his body disappears into the ocean but his spirit finds an empty shell in which to live. Some of these shells are washed ashore, and our souls are released back into the world."

"Is it a true story?" asks Nick.

"I don't know," says Porquoix. "It may have happened to me, but I can't remember. That's the mystery. Nobody can recall exactly what takes place immediately after they die and before they become an arora. It's like a dream that fades away."

"What about the wings?" asks Nick. "Why does the shell have wings?"

"There are different stories about that," says Porquoix. "Some say it is a symbol of the birds that migrate through Ilhas dos Fantasmas. They come and go like restless spirits. Others believe that once, long ago, there actually was a conch shell with wings. A fisherman found it on the beach, but when he tried to pick it up, it flew away, high into the clouds. Nobody knows the truth, though every child on Prithvideep has this symbol tattooed on his or her cheek as a sign of good luck."

"I wish I had a tattoo," says Nick.

Porquoix laughs. "But you weren't born here."

"I wish I was."

"Well, I can give you a tattoo. I know how it's done. All I need is a needle and ink."

"Tomorrow?"

"Remember, it hurts a lot."

"I don't care," says Nick.

The next day, when the two friends meet again, Nick brings a needle from his mother's sewing box and a bottle of ink from his father's desk. Sitting inside the grotto, a shaft of sunlight illuminating Nick's cheek, Porquoix pierces his friend's skin again and again, outlining the shape of a conch shell with wings. It is painful, each prick of the needle like a thorn, blood mixing with the ink. When he is done, Nick looks at his reflection in a tidal pool, then smiles at his friend.

Later, when he goes home, his mother screams when she sees the mark on his face and calls him a "heathen savage," and "a pagan brute."

"It's just a tattoo," says Nick.

"Look at you!" his mother cries. "Such a fair and handsome face. You've scarred it for life."

"But everyone on Prithvideep has a tattoo," he says.

"Nicodemus! Nicodemus! How could you do this to us?" his mother wails. "What will they say when we go home to Massachusetts?"

"I don't want to go home," he says. "I like it here."

Hezekiah Osgood is outraged and punishes his son for getting the tattoo—twenty strokes of a bamboo cane and three hours of copying passages from Pliny's *Historia Naturalis*. As soon as he is done, however, Nick goes back to playing with Porquoix.

His parents disapprove of his friendship. They forbid him to meet Porquoix, but the two remain inseparable and meet in secret. As the years pass, Nick grows older and taller than Porquoix. The age of an arora never changes, but a boy matures. It hardly matters to the two of them; they enjoy each other's company regardless of their age. Though Porquoix keeps his distance from the water, he teaches Nick how to fish and tells him the secrets of the reef, the places where lobsters hide and how to sail a catamaran and bait his hooks with live eels to catch the largest tuna.

Nick and his parents remain on the island for nearly twenty years, and he never imagines that he will ever have to leave. He pays no attention to his father's books and experiments, preferring the open sea and beaches to the stuffy rooms in which his parents live. One day, as Nick and Porquoix are sitting beside each other on a rock near the Osgoods' bungalow, they notice Nick's father come outside. He is carrying a heavy camera attached to a tripod, which he sets up in front of his son. As Porquoix turns to leave, Professor Osgood calls out.

"No, wait," he says. "Don't go. I want to take your photograph. Both of you together."

The two friends are puzzled, but Porquoix takes his seat again and watches as Nick's father positions the camera and focuses the lens. Then the professor puts his head under the black hood and holds up the magnesium flash. Porquoix and Nick stare at the camera self-consciously when Hezekiah orders them to smile.

A blinding burst of white light is accompanied by an acrid cloud of smoke. The flash tears them apart. And from that day onward, Nick is left alone. He has never felt such a terrible loss, and for days he wanders about the island in tears, searching for his friend. Not a trace of the arora remains. Though he continues to play the thumb piano every day, Porquoix never returns. As his grief turns to anger, Nick realizes what his father has done. He will never forgive him, not in this life or the next.

33

The sailboat was over thirty feet long, with a mast that rose at least that high. Black pennants fluttered in the breeze, and a funeral wreath with velvet ribbons hung from the bowsprit. The bleached white sail swelled as a breeze gusted across the bay and the boat rocked against its moorings. Seagulls wheeled and dived overhead. The lighthouse stood out against the horizon—a squat white tower—like a chess piece that never moved.

At exactly 4:00, a gleaming black hearse came down the street toward the dock, driving slowly with its headlights on. The hearse pulled up in the harbor parking lot, and Enoch Knox stepped out of the driver's seat. He was dressed as he always was, in a long black coat buttoned over a charcoal suit, starched white shirt, and a dark gray tie. The only difference from his usual attire was a captain's hat that he fitted on his head, which gave him a nautical air. Meanwhile, the four pallbearers, also dressed in matching black suits, emerged from the hearse and solemnly opened the rear doors.

There were only a few people along the waterfront, a pair of fishermen hosing off their boat, and a cluster of tourists who stood by respectfully to watch the ceremony. The only mourners were Alma and Ted Parker, as well as Courtney, Ming, and Orion.

Shouldering the casket, the pallbearers proceeded slowly forward, walking in step. Their dark trousers moved in unison, as if they were an eight-legged creature, a giant spider, its hard, rectangular body with polished brass handles and knobs. No music accompanied the procession, only the cries of gulls and the rhythmic flapping of the canvas sail. Yet the ceremony had a dignified simplicity as the casket was carried onto the dock, up a gangway, and placed in the bow of the ship.

Watching the funeral procession, Ming couldn't help but feel sad, even though she hadn't known Nick Osgood. Looking across at Orion, she saw him wipe away a tear with his sleeve. They had decided not to accompany the casket out to sea, preferring to say farewell from the dock.

The pallbearers took up their positions as crew. Enoch Knox stood behind the wheel as one of the black-suited men scrambled up the riggings to unfurl a second sail, with a diagonal black stripe. Two of the others untied the ropes and waited for a signal to cast off, while the fourth helped steady the casket, which rocked back and forth with the uneven motion of the waves, a mortal cargo that would soon be consigned to the sea.

As the boat slipped free of the dock and the sail bulged with the wind, it seemed as if this moment was happening nearly a hundred years ago, when Nick Osgood and his parents had first set sail from Hornswoggle Bay on their way to Prithvideep. The high sea wall blocked a view of the ocean beyond, except for a narrow passage that opened onto the vast expanse of the Atlantic. The sailboat headed out across choppy water, slowly at first, then catching a steadier breeze. As the sail tilted with the wind, the pallbearers leaned out over the gunwales, their black suits like four exclamation marks against the white spray.

After they had watched the sailboat disappear beyond the headland where the lighthouse stood, Ted Parker took Alma's arm, and they walked back toward their car. Orion, Ming, and Courtney followed silently, all of them moved by the solemn ceremony. But when they reached the edge of the dock, a familiar figure was leaning against a pile of lobster traps. Nick Osgood didn't seem at all upset by his own funeral. Instead he had a look of amusement on his face as he pointed to one of the shops along the waterfront. It had a white clapboard facade with a sagging roof, where Nick's Bait and Tackle once stood. Now the shop wore a fresh coat of paint and had a new sign out front.

HORNSWOGGLE ANTIQUES

BUY A PIECE OF OLDE NEW ENGLAND

34

When he went back to the library the next day, Orion picked up one of the books he had found earlier, *Operation Johnny Rook*. Though he was supposed to be helping Ms. Parker solve the riddle of the ghosts and doing research on Ilhas dos Fantasmas, he found himself distracted by the spy novel. The story was about an atom bomb lost in the middle of Antarctica. If it exploded, the bomb would destroy most of the southern hemisphere. The hero was a British secret agent stationed on the Falkland Islands. Every time Orion opened the book, he turned to the last page to see how the arora was doing. (Though he could have read the ending of the novel, Orion resisted the temptation.) The arora greeted him with a mock salute, then carried on with his game of mumblety-peg, touching the pocketknife to his shoulder or elbow and flicking it to the ground. Orion knew exactly how he felt, going through the repetitive motions of a game, just to pass the time. The boy seemed completely bored inside the book, even if it was an exciting thriller.

That evening at dinner, Orion ended up telling his parents what was happening at the library. He hadn't planned to do it, but his mother had heard about the demonstration at the library from one of the other parents. When she mentioned Mrs. Hokum's name, Orion rolled his eyes.

"You shouldn't be that way about your teacher," said his mother, passing him a bowl of carrots and peas.

"She's just a stupid witch," said Orion.

"Don't talk like that," his father said. "Aren't you going to have any vegetables?"

"No."

"No, thank you," his mother corrected him sternly.

"Okay, no, thank you."

"You should really have some peas and carrots," his mother said.

"But you just told me to say 'no, thank you.'"

"Don't get smart, young man," his father said. "What was the demonstration about?"

"Mrs. Hokum thinks there are dangerous books in the library, just because Marigold Deitz got scared while we were doing our social studies report," said Orion. "Mrs. Hokum burned one of the books, but she doesn't know the truth about the ghosts. . . ."

He stopped himself, though it was too late. His parents looked at him suspiciously.

"What ghosts?" his father said.

"Um . . . nothing."

"Orion?" his mother said in a serious voice.

Realizing that he didn't have much choice, and knowing they would probably find out soon enough, he told his parents the whole story—except for the parts about sneaking into the library and the funeral home. He explained how they were doing a final report on Ilhas dos Fantasmas for social studies, and how Ming had found a book called *The Compleat Necromancer*, and other books containing the arora. He described how they'd seen Nick Osgood's ghost in the cemetery and about the thumb piano made from a skull. When Orion finally finished, the mashed potatoes on his plate had gone cold and the gravy had congealed into a thick brown puddle.

Orion's mother stared at him in alarm, then looked at her husband.

"I told you we shouldn't have let him play those video games!" she said.

"He needs to see a psychiatrist," his father concluded, shaking his head.

By Monday afternoon, Orion had an appointment with Dr. Pifflegeist. His mother picked him up right after school and drove him straight to the psychiatrist's office.

"Mom, I don't need to see a shrink!" he said.

"It's all right, Orion," she said, patting his arm. "Try not to get nervous."

"I'm not," he said. "I just wish you'd believe me."

"Of course I do. Of course."

"Mom, there really are ghosts in the library. You can ask Ms. Parker."

"I don't think we need to bother her," his mother said. "We don't want to start any rumors, do we?"

"But I'm not crazy!"

"Of course you're not. I'm sure that Dr. Pifflegeist will be able to set you straight." Then she looked at him sternly and added, "Your father and I have agreed that you're not to play any more video games."

"That doesn't have anything to do with it. The ghosts are inside library books."

"Of course they are," his mother said.

"Mom, it's a waste of time taking me to a shrink."

"I wish you'd stop calling him that," his mother said as they pulled into a parking lot of the medical center. "Dr. Pifflegeist is a distinguished psychiatrist. He specializes in adolescent mental health."

Reluctantly, Orion followed his mother into the building and up the stairs to the doctor's office, where three other patients waited patiently.

When Orion was finally called inside, he was surprised to see that Dr. Pifflegeist was shorter than he—about four feet tall, with a round face and a gray goatee. *The shrink must have shrunk,* Orion told himself, trying to keep a straight face. Dr. Pifflegeist's clothes looked as if they were too tight on him, the jacket of his suit riding up his arms and his trouser cuffs three inches above his ankles. Shaking hands with Orion, the psychiatrist pointed to a leather armchair in the corner.

"What's going on? Your mother says it's an emergency." Dr. Pifflegeist spoke abruptly, in a taut voice. His eyes, which were like green marbles, remained locked on his patient, who shifted uneasily in the chair.

"It's nothing, really," Orion said. "My parents think I'm insane, but I'm not. You see, my friends and I found these ghosts in the library. . . ."

He hesitated to see how the psychiatrist would respond, but the eyes never wavered.

"Go on," said Dr. Pifflegeist.

"There was this professor . . . Hezekiah Osgood, who went to study primitive cultures on some islands in the Indian Ocean. He discovered a kind of ghost called *arora,* and trapped them inside his books. I know it sounds crazy but it's true."

"And how does that make you feel?" asked Dr. Pifflegeist.

"I don't know," said Orion.

"Are you afraid of ghosts?"

"Not really. Not anymore."

The two green marbles hadn't moved, and Orion wondered if Dr. Pifflegeist ever closed his eyes.

"How long has it been since you started seeing these ghosts?" the psychiatrist asked.

"About four days."

"And they only appear inside books?"

"Most of them, except for one. Nick Osgood's ghost. He wanders around."

For half an hour, Dr. Pifflegeist kept questioning Orion about what was happening at school and the video games he liked to play. But most of the questions led back to the ghosts, and the psychiatrist's eyes never left him, except when he glanced at the clock on the wall.

"Have you ever been hypnotized?" the doctor asked when their time was almost up.

Orion shook his head.

"As far as I can tell, there's nothing seriously wrong with you. But I'm going to try hypnosis," said Dr. Pifflegeist. "That way I can dispel any illusions you might have about ghosts."

Orion wasn't sure he liked the idea of being hypnotized, but it didn't seem as if he had much choice.

"Don't worry, it won't hurt. Just look at my eyes and try to relax."

Orion felt as if the green marbles were about to pop out of the psychiatrist's head. He wanted to look away, but he couldn't, as he felt himself being pulled into their glassy orbit, as if he were spinning around and around like water draining out of a sink, as if all of his thoughts were being siphoned from his brain.

Seconds later he woke up, as the doctor snapped his stubby fingers. Nothing seemed to have changed. The psychiatrist's eyes hadn't blinked. The same pictures and certificates were on the walls. Orion glanced down at his feet and saw the ornate patterns in the carpet.

"Now, do you believe in ghosts?"

Orion looked up at Dr. Pifflegeist, puzzled by the question.

"No," he said, and shook his head. "Of course not."

35

"*A remac a deen ew.*"

It took Alma a minute to find a pencil and a piece of paper so that she could write down what Nick had said and then reverse the letters.

"What for?" she asked.

"We need a camera to take pictures of the ghosts," Nick explained, pausing after every phrase so that Alma could decipher his words. "That's how my father trapped them in the books. He took their photographs and then projected the images onto the pages. If we can reverse the process, maybe we'll be able to set them free."

Alma glanced around the darkened library. No one else was there. It was six o'clock, Monday evening, and she had sent her assistants home before locking the doors. Here she was, sitting alone with a ghost, trying to figure out how to break a supernatural spell. A week ago, if someone had told her this was going to happen, she would have laughed in their face. But now there wasn't much to laugh about. Roberta Hokum had circulated a petition demanding that the selectmen in Carville call a special town meeting to discuss the problem. The hearing was going to be held tomorrow night at the library, and Alma had been asked to explain what was going on. She knew there were rumors running through the town, mostly spread by Roberta. Some people believed that Alma had been ordering objectionable books. Some were saying the library was infested with rats and other vermin. There were even a few who thought she was using the money from library fines to subscribe to underground magazines and journals.

Out of curiosity, a lot more people had come to the library today than usual. Whenever they looked at Alma, she could see the suspicion on their faces. One man she'd never seen before kept snooping around the current periodicals, flipping through newspapers and magazines as if he were looking for evidence of a crime. A woman with frizzy red hair, whom Alma recognized from the demonstration, spent several hours going through the card catalog and making lists of titles. When one of the assistants tried to show her how to use the computer, the woman got flustered and left. Others were lurking about in the stacks, pretending to browse for books but actually hoping to find something else. Even the youngest children seemed nervous, holding their parents' hands when they came inside the library and not making a sound as they sat on the cushions in the reading area. At first, Alma thought she was imagining things, but after a while she understood that the townspeople were watching her with judgmental eyes.

If only they knew the truth.

The librarian heard a loud knock at the door and looked up in surprise to see Courtney peering in through the glass. Alma went across and let her in.

"What are you doing here?" Alma asked. "I thought you were grounded."

"Well, my mom heard about what was going on. She thinks it's terrible that Mrs. Hokum is trying to ban some of the books in the library," said Courtney. "I told her you might need some help, and she said I could come over for a couple of hours."

"I'm glad you're here," said Alma, "We've got a problem. Nick says we need a camera to get the ghosts out of the books."

Until then, Courtney hadn't noticed Nick, and she nodded hello as the ghost waved a pale hand.

"I have an old camera at home," said Courtney. "But it doesn't take very good pictures, and I don't think I have any film. But how is a camera going to help?"

They both looked at Nick, who scribbled his answer on a piece of paper.

"*Arora hcae hpargotohp ot deen ew. Segap eht ffo thgil rieht leep ot.*"

While Alma was translating what Nick said, Courtney looked around the darkened library.

"What about that?" she said, pointing to the photocopying machine.

The librarian gave her a skeptical frown. "That machine never works!" Alma said.

"Let's give it a try," said Courtney, turning to Nick. "What do you think?"

Nick smiled enthusiastically, then searched through the piles of books on Alma's desk and found *A Comprehensive History of*

American Whaling Vessels. He opened it and grinned when he saw Porquoix's face looking up at him.

"Wait, we'll need a dime," said Alma, searching through her purse. She had quarters and nickels and pennies but no dimes. Opening her desk, she found paper clips, a Canadian quarter, half a dozen rubber bands, and finally a single dime, hidden beneath a stack of envelopes.

She and Courtney approached the photocopier with trepidation, not sure what was going to happen. Nick took a few steps back, still holding Porquoix's image in his hands. The machine had been switched off, and Alma had to turn it on again. The photocopier made a purring noise, followed by a rattle, as it warmed up. Lights flickered on the control panel and it beeped twice, then shuddered as if it were trying to wake itself up. Alma and Courtney waited impatiently as Nick looked down at his friend.

"I hope this won't hurt," he said to Porquoix.

"It can't be worse than being eaten by a shark," replied Porquoix with a brave smile.

The photocopier rumbled, a low volcanic sound, after which a green light came on. Alma's hand was shaking as she fed the dime into the slot and adjusted the brightness to the highest level. Nick handed Courtney the book, and she opened the photocopier's lid and carefully positioned Porquoix's image facedown on the glass, making sure the spine of the book wouldn't get damaged. Then she pressed lightly on the cover and punched the green button.

There was a flash of light, bright as a welding torch, and a groaning noise as the rollers and gears inside the machine began to turn. Courtney held her breath as the light moved across the page, then stopped. A second later, there was a creaking sound as the photocopier spat out a piece of paper. When Courtney picked it up, the sheet was blank.

"May I speak with Orion, please?" said Ming.

"Hold on a moment," his mother said. "He's in his room. I'll call him."

"Thanks. . . ."

"Hey." Orion's voice sounded sleepy.

"It's me," said Ming.

"Yeah."

"Is everything okay?"

"Sure. Everything's fine," said Orion.

"What about the shrink? How did that go?"

"It was okay. Nothing serious."

"So, we need to finish our report," said Ming. "We've only got another week until the World's Fair. We need to make posters and put together a display."

"Let's work on it tomorrow after school. At the library," said Orion. He didn't sound like himself.

"Will your parents let you go?" Ming asked.

"Sure, why not?"

"Aren't they worried?" said Ming.

"Why?"

"You know . . . the ghosts."

"What are you talking about?"

"Orion! You're being weird."

"You're the one that's being weird, talking about ghosts."

"Come on, quit it. I spoke to Courtney about an hour ago. She's gone to the library to help Ms. Parker. They still haven't figured out how to get the arora out of those books, and tomorrow there's a town meeting at the library."

"What's an arora?"

"Very funny, Orion. This is serious."

"I'm being serious," he said, annoyed.

"No, you're not."

"Ming, I'm totally serious. I don't know what you're talking about."

"Yeah, and now you're going to tell me you never saw Nick Osgood's ghost and never went inside the funeral home that night we found the thumb piano."

"Huh?"

"Okay. Forget it. I'm hanging up, Orion. I don't have time for this."

"All right. But I still don't know why you expect me to believe in ghosts."

"Good night."

"See you. 'Night."

Courtney and Alma stared at the blank sheet of paper, not sure what to think. They glanced up at Nick, who had a worried look on his face. He had moved away from the photocopier and stood in front of a shelf of dictionaries and encyclopedias.

Nervously, Courtney lifted the cover of the machine and

removed the book. When she turned it over, all she could see were paragraphs of ink. Porquoix's image had disappeared. Courtney kept turning the pages to make sure he wasn't there, but the book was empty except for words. By this time, Nick had taken a few steps closer, peering over her shoulder at the printed text and the plain white sheet of paper that came out of the photocopier. He was afraid to think what must have happened to Porquoix, remembering the blinding flash of light from his father's camera so many years ago. In that burning instant the two of them had been separated, and now he wondered if Porquoix were lost forever.

Alma shook her head dejectedly as the photocopier let out a mechanical sigh.

"Onaip bmuht eht yrt!" said Nick, refusing to give up hope.

Before Courtney and Alma were able to decipher what Nick had said, he rushed across to her office and gestured toward the locked drawer of her desk. Without much hope, the librarian took out her key and removed the skull. Two vacant eyes stared back at her, and the yellowed teeth were clenched together in a painful grimace. Courtney watched Alma with a worried expression as she touched a key with her right thumb and played a note. Now that the photocopier had stopped, the library was completely silent. One note followed the next, like beads of sound being strung on a musical thread. It was a mournful tune, and Nick Osgood's eyes were full of tears.

All at once there was a rustling in the shadows, as if someone had brushed against the rack of newspapers. Alma blinked with surprise, still plucking at the metal tines. Courtney spun around, seeing a movement near the office door, like the headlight of a passing car reflecting off the window. Nick had also sensed a presence, and he turned his head. Another flicker of light played against the wall, then gradually came into focus—the figure of a teenage boy. Porquoix stood in front of them, squinting his eyes and holding out both arms as if to balance himself.

He looked about for the source of the sound, nodding at Alma and Courtney, before he caught sight of his childhood friend. The old man approached him and reached out, smiling with delight as their hands clasped.

36

Ted Parker had been wondering why his wife hadn't come home from the library yet when the phone began to ring, and it was Alma on the line.

"Ted, I want you to get over here right away," she said, "and bring as many dimes as you can find."

"Dimes?"

"Yes, there should be a bunch of them in the drawer where we keep the car keys. And look in the glass jar on my bedside table, where I put all my change. We'll need about fifty."

"What for?" said Ted.

"Don't worry, I'll explain when you get here," said Alma. "Please hurry!"

There was a Red Sox game on TV that Ted wanted to watch, but he knew this was more important. Though he still had his doubts about the ghosts and was searching for some sort of scientific explanation, Ted understood that there were things that even chemistry couldn't reveal.

He gathered up as many dimes as he could and put them all in a plastic bag before driving over to the library. When he got there, Ted was surprised to find that his wife wasn't alone.

"You remember Courtney, don't you?" Alma said, as she let her husband in the main door. "She's the one who first found the arora, and these are two of our friends."

Never having been introduced to a ghost before, Ted didn't know exactly what to do. He shook hands with Courtney, but when it came to Nick and Porquoix, he made do with a quick nod of his head. The spirits returned his greeting as Alma began to explain what was going on. Before long, all of them were working together, carrying the books from the librarian's office to the photocopier. As Courtney positioned the next arora to be scanned and Alma put a dime in the machine, Ted Parker held the thumb piano in his hands. He knew how to play the guitar and often said that if he hadn't become a chemistry teacher, he would have joined a rock band. As soon as the image was exposed, Ted picked at the keys, improvising a version of an old Rolling Stones' song, "Under My Thumb."

The arora that appeared a few moments later was Sheikh Rustom Ibn Fanous al Ifrit. He made his entrance from behind the photocopier, as if he had just stepped out of the machine. Adjusting his turban, the sheikh greeted the others by placing one hand over his heart. In the other hand he carried his water pipe. Though the library had NO SMOKING signs on the walls, Alma decided not to point these out to the ghost as he settled himself in a chair. The pipe gurgled when Sheikh Rustom drew in a deep puff, and the smoke trickled out between his lips, but there wasn't the faintest smell of burning tobacco, and the pale fumes vanished in the air like cobwebs dissolving in a breeze.

"Once all of the ghosts are released, where are they going to go?" asked Courtney.

Alma hadn't thought that far ahead, but she figured the arora would stay inside the library and make themselves invisible when anyone else appeared. Her main concern was to get the ghosts out of the books before the town meeting tomorrow night.

One by one, they continued to photocopy the pages until there were more than two dozen spirits gathered in the room. Ted kept playing the thumb piano, trying out different tunes like "Blue Suede Shoes" and "Purple Haze." The arora seemed drawn to his music, especially the younger ones, who sat in a circle around him and even clapped their hands after a rendition of "Yellow Submarine." As each phantom appeared, looking bewildered and confused, Nick welcomed them into the library and explained what was going on. After having been trapped inside the books for so many years, they were all unsteady on their feet, like sailors stepping onto land after months at sea. They looked about their unfamiliar surroundings nervously, seeing the dark beams overhead and bookshelves against the walls, wondering where the coconut palms had gone, the golden sands of Prithvideep. Though more than half a century had passed since they were trapped inside the books, it felt as if they had been instantly snatched from one world into the next.

Courtney set aside the books that were empty. By now she had two large piles, though there were still at least another twenty remaining. As she picked up the next volume, the title caught her eye—A *Statistical Analysis of the Maritime Trade.* As Courtney opened it, she recognized the dark-haired woman—Nalini. Their eyes met for a moment, and Courtney gave her a reassuring smile before placing the image facedown on the glass. The process had become automatic now as the librarian slid a dime into the slot. With a reluctant wheeze and rattle, the photocopier began to work, but just when Courtney expected the flash of light, there was a gnashing of gears and a groaning of belts. The photocopier shuddered twice and then stood still. A red light blinked on the control panel and the digital display flashed a message:

SYSTEM MALFUNCTION
CALL SERVICE TECHNICIAN

"No! Not now! I can't believe this is happening," said Alma, resisting an urge to kick the machine.

Removing the book, Courtney saw that Nalini was still there on the page, looking more puzzled than ever. At least the machine hadn't swallowed her image or mangled her ghost in a tortured paper jam. Alma tried all the tricks she knew to make the photocopier work—opening the front cover and closing it again, pressing the Reset button a dozen times, then turning the whole thing off and starting it again. Nothing happened, and with a sinking feeling she realized that they would have to wait until the next day to call the technician. After Ted stopped playing the thumb piano, most of the arora dispersed, finding nooks and crevices within the library where they could hide. Only Nick and Porquoix remained. When Alma explained what was wrong, they nodded in disappointment, then turned aside and vanished.

37

After the photocopier stopped working, Ted and Alma dropped Courtney at home. Her mother had gone to the movies with some friends, and she was glad to be alone. It was too late to call Ming or Orion.

Leaning close to her dresser mirror and using an extra-fine-point pen, Courtney carefully traced an outline on her cheek—a conch shell with wings. The indelible blue ink seemed too dark at first, and it was difficult to get the shape just right, but she worked slowly, carefully, as if she were giving herself a real tattoo. The wings were the hardest part to draw. She had copied the symbol from one of the bookplates onto a piece of paper, and taped it to a corner of the mirror so she wouldn't make any mistakes.

After she was done, Courtney waited for the ink to dry. When she looked in the mirror again, a few minutes later, she thought of Nalini, who had the same tattoo on her cheek. Courtney felt a kinship with the arora, as if she were recalling an image of herself from a previous birth—an earlier incarnation.

But more than anything, Courtney just liked the look of the

tattoo. It made her feel as if she were one of the ghosts. She knew that after she washed her face a couple of times and the ink began to fade, it would look even more authentic. Maybe someday she'd actually get a tattoo—one that would never rub off.

Agnes watched her from the foot of the bed and wagged her tail.

"What are you looking at?" said Courtney.

The golden retriever kept staring at her as if she were eyeing the tattoo.

"Agnes, what do you think you were in your last life?" said Courtney. "A cocker spaniel? Or a chihuahua? Maybe a Doberman pinscher."

The dog's tail slapped against the covers of the bed.

"I wonder if dogs have ghosts."

The next morning, Courtney and Ming met near the sixth-grade lockers a few minutes before class.

"I like your tattoo," said Ming.

"Yeah. My mother freaked out this morning," said Courtney, laughing. "She thought it was real. But listen, I've got to tell you what happened last night. . . ."

As Courtney described how the ghosts had been released from the books, Ming's eyes got wider and wider.

"We need to go back to the library today right after school and help set the rest of them free," said Courtney.

"Don't worry, I'll be there," Ming said.

Just then they saw Orion coming down the hall.

"Hey," he said, squinting at Courtney. "What's that on your face?"

"Don't you recognize it?"

"No," he said.

"It's that symbol the arora have tattooed on their cheeks," said Courtney.

"*Arora?*"

"You know, the spirits inside the books," said Ming.

"What is this," he said, "early Halloween?"

"Don't tell me you're still playing that game?" said Ming. "Come on, Orion. You know what we're talking about!"

"Sure. *Ghosts,*" Orion said sarcastically, raising his hands and waving his fingers. "Woooooooooo . . ."

"What's wrong with you?" said Courtney.

"He was like this on the phone last night," said Ming. "I think he's just trying to be annoying."

"Next thing you'll be telling me there are skeletons in the lockers and witches on broomsticks," said Orion.

"Stop kidding around. This isn't a joke."

"Boo!" said Orion, laughing.

"What's your problem?" said Courtney. "You know exactly what we're talking about."

"Yeah. Spirits. Phantoms. Spooky things that walk through walls and dress up in sheets." Orion shook his head. "I'm not falling for this. Give it up, you guys."

At that moment the bell began to ring and everyone started rushing to class.

"Forget it," said Courtney. "We'll prove it to you this afternoon."

38

While most of the escaping spirits take refuge inside the library, hiding in the stacks, between the folded pages of old newspapers, or behind posters on the walls, one of the arora ventures outside.

D'Kele is among the first to be released. Passing through the photocopier, he feels as if he has been shaved off the page by a razor of light. After his image peels away from the paper, D'Kele finds himself able to move about again, no longer trapped in a cage of words.

His first instinct is to search for Nalini. Unable to find her among the other ghosts who have been released, D'Kele calls out her name, but he receives no reply. He searches through the stacks and even ascends to the library attic, full of boxes of paper, but there is no sign of his beloved. She is still captive in her book. The music of the thumb piano cannot soothe D'Kele's restless spirit as he struggles to understand where he is, disoriented and afraid. The thick granite walls of the library seem to lean in upon him, and the plaintive melody echoes off the high ceilings. He listens in vain for the familiar sound of the surf washing against the beaches of Prithvideep and the rustling of palm fronds stirring in the night air, the restless calls of migrating birds.

Slipping out of a window, D'Kele makes his way to the giant oak that grows behind the library. He has never seen a tree like this before, so deeply rooted in the soil, with a massive trunk that rises up to a leafy crown. It is unlike anything that grows on Prithvideep—the slender coconut palms, or the guava and gum trees, hardly taller than a man. Climbing up through the scaffolding of branches, D'Kele moves cautiously, for he is still unsteady after his long confinement. There is no wind, but the oak limbs seem to sway precariously, and the leaves dance like shadows agitated by a flickering candle flame. D'Kele finally reaches the top of the oak, emerging through a dome of foliage and looking up at the stars.

The old light, which has traveled through space for years, bathes him in its glow. D'Kele feels its ancient radiance as he scans the heavens to learn the truth.

But the night sky over Carville is opaque, and the galaxies are smudged by light from towns and cities on earth. Even from the top of the tree, D'Kele has difficulty reading the night sky. The few stars he recognizes seem out of place, the constellations reversed and misaligned, like a scrambled alphabet. D'Kele has always been able to see the future in the stars, but tonight the answers appear illegible and obscure. He glances about and sees the lighthouse beacon, a bright finger pointing out into the oceanic night.

As a star-catcher, D'Kele is able to translate the distant messages that travel as waves of light, preserving them on the sacred scrolls of bark cloth. Long before it happens, he knows that the Final Extinction is coming, when the arora vanish from Ilhas dos Fantasmas. He understands the dangers of the professor's camera, with its sinister glass eye and black veil. He has a premonition of the searing flash that steals Nalini away from him, just as it captures the other arora. D'Kele knows the threat, and he tries to warn the spirits. He anxiously watches as the professor empties the Isle of Banished Spirits before turning his lens on the other phantoms. D'Kele tries to protect the gum trees that Osgood destroys for his experiments. One by one the *Glutinous luminosa* are cut down until none are left. The bark is stripped away and boiled into an emulsion that the professor uses to capture the ghosts on his photographic plates.

All of this is written and predicted on the star-catcher's scrolls that foretell the professor's malicious designs. D'Kele knows that the ghosts will be trapped and taken to a foreign land, where they will be imprisoned within a crypt of books. All of this is revealed in the star-catcher's charts, but he is forbidden to tell anyone these truths. Yet now, as he stares up at the blurred confusion of an unfamiliar sky, D'Kele cannot decipher his fate.

The service technician arrived the next day at 2:20 in the afternoon, and it took him an hour to repair the photocopier. He told Alma that he couldn't promise how much longer it would keep working. ("You really need to buy a new machine," he said.) But after a couple of belts and one of the switches had been replaced, the photocopier seemed to be functioning again. At 3:30, Ming,

Orion, and Courtney arrived, and they worked on their social studies report until 5:00, when the library closed. Ted Parker joined them soon afterward, and together they quickly carried the remaining books out of Alma's office. The town meeting was scheduled for 7:00 that evening.

Orion was puzzled by all of the urgency, not knowing what was going on. Whenever he asked his friends for an explanation, they scowled at him, as if he should have known the answer. Ming and Courtney kept talking about ghosts, as if they really existed, and Orion couldn't understand why they were acting so weird. He certainly didn't believe in ghosts, especially not in a library. It was crazy to think that the place was haunted, but even Mr. and Ms. Parker seemed to believe it was true. They looked at Orion as if he were the only one who was deluded.

"All right," said Ming as she put down a stack of books on the table. "You really don't believe in ghosts?"

Orion shook his head.

"Then take a look at this," she said, handing him a book from the pile.

He shrugged and opened it. There was nothing but words on the page. He read a couple lines out loud:

" 'The economic benefits of the whaling industry extend far beyond the eastern coast of the United States, affecting other parts of the country . . .' "

Ming interrupted him. "Can't you see her?"

"Who?" said Orion.

"The arora. She's right there."

"No, she isn't."

By this time Courtney had joined them.

"So, now are you convinced?" she asked.

"What's there to be convinced about? It's just an old book about economics or something."

Orion stared at the printed page, wondering if his friends had gone crazy.

"The ghost is looking straight at you," said Ming.

"If she is, I can't see her," said Orion, turning the book upside down and shaking it, then giving it back to Ming. "Anyway, I'm going home. I've had enough of this. You guys can play your games without me."

"Wait," said Courtney. "Give him the thumb piano."

Ming ran to get the skull from Ms. Parker's office, and when she brought it out, Orion made a face.

"That's disgusting," he said.

"You're the one that found it," said Ming. "Why don't you try to play a tune?"

Orion shook his head.

"Go on," said Courtney. "Are you scared?"

Reluctantly, Orion took the skull in both hands. Holding it away from himself, he flicked one of the keys with his thumb. The note was high-pitched, at the upper end of the scale. It was followed by a lower note, the vibrations mingling in an eerie harmony. Orion remembered hearing the sound before, and all at once he felt the hypnosis lifting, as if Dr. Pifflegeist's eyes had finally blinked. As he kept playing the notes, the ghosts came out of hiding, emerging from the stacks and sliding out from behind the posters on the walls. They were drawn to the music as if a magnetic force were emanating from the metal tines. As the host of spirits gathered in the room, Orion could clearly see them now, and he remembered the arora, as if the music had restored their presence. Everything came flooding back into his mind.

On the far side of the library, Orion saw Tarquin. He was standing apart from the others with the pocketknife in his hand. Catching Orion's eye, the arora gave a mock salute, then folded the blade of his knife away and put it in his pocket, as if the game of mumblety-peg were finally over. Meanwhile, Ming had met Cziczee, the girl with the pigtails, who had been trapped inside the envelope. The two of them were gesturing and laughing, trying to make themselves understood. As Orion kept on playing the thumb piano, the arora took Ming by the hand and spun her around. The library began to feel a bit like a party as the spirits were reunited, greeting one another after years of separation.

The sound of Orion's playing filters out through the windows and skylights of the library, to the top of the oak, where D'Kele sits alone. He hears the trickle of notes and feels their current pulling him back into the building. At first he resists their call, but as the music continues, he descends through the leaves and down the ladder of branches, slipping across the lawn and through the window.

He sees the other arora and the librarian standing near the machine, as well as the boy playing the thumb piano. D'Kele distrusts the music for what it has done to the ghosts, luring them into captivity, but now it seems as if the same notes are guiding them to freedom. As he watches, Courtney takes a book from the table and places it inside the machine. Alma drops a coin into the slot and presses a button. D'Kele flinches at the sudden burst of light, keeping himself hidden behind a curtain.

Three more notes flow out of the skull, each one higher than the next—like the trill of a bird. And then he sees Nalini. She appears at the top of the stairs leading down to the stacks. Nalini looks about her in bewilderment, trying to comprehend her surroundings. Courtney is the first person she recognizes, and Nalini reaches out to touch her face, running her fingers over the ink tattoo and smiling. Over the past few days they have looked at each other so often it seems as if they have known each other forever.

Nalini's image wavers as she struggles to keep her balance, but when D'Kele calls her name, she steadies herself and searches for him with her eyes. Sweeping aside the curtain, he rushes to her, and before she knows it, D'Kele holds her in his arms. Still trembling from the shock of being torn off the page, Nalini embraces her lover. She has waited so long for this moment, though it feels as if only a few minutes have passed since they were separated—moments that stretch back into hours, into days and years.

39

Though the photocopier grumbled and complained, it did not break down again. By 6:45, the last ghost had been released and the books were carried back into Alma's office. The thumb piano was locked safely away, and the spirits disappeared into their hiding places. Five minutes later, the selectmen began to arrive for the town meeting. Orion, Ming, and Courtney helped arrange the chairs and set up a table at the front. Word of the special meeting had spread through Carville, and more and more people arrived until there was standing room only. At 7:15, the chairman called the meeting to order. He mumbled a brief statement about "serious allegations," then invited Roberta Hokum to speak. When she stood up, several people clapped.

Roberta had bought herself a new outfit for the occasion, a pink sweater that matched the color of her nails and a yellow dress that looked so cheerful it made Orion wince. Ming nudged him as their teacher smiled, the same false look of glee with which she faced her students.

"Good evening," she said, her voice as sweet as cough syrup. "Thank you all for coming here tonight. This is a very important meeting because it has to do with something terribly dear to my heart. This is about the young people of Carville. Our children. Our students. Our future. We must protect and nurture them. We must show them the best things in life. We must make them smile...."

Her lipstick formed a perfect crease as the corners of her mouth curled up. For another five minutes, Mrs. Hokum carried on about her philosophy of "positive thinking" and how she believed in "good minds and good deeds." Then she took a deep breath and paused, looking around the library before fixing her eyes on Alma Parker, accusingly.

Orion leaned over to Ming. Under his breath he said, "I wish there was a remote control to switch her off."

Ming nodded. "I can't believe anyone listens to her."

Mrs. Hokum turned to look in their direction and droned on, "Unfortunately, there are those who do not share our constructive vision but prefer to dwell on the negative things in life. When we see light, they see darkness. When we see joy, they see suffering. When we look forward to a bright future for our children, they look back into the dismal shadows of the past. Here in this very library, we have books that are full of cynicism and doubt, books that question the good things in life, books that cast a specter on our happy town. We must not let these books get into the hands of our children. These books frighten them with disheartening visions of despair. Instead of uplifting their readers with joy and hope, the authors of these books choose to drag them down into dismal and dispiriting subjects. I believe that we should remove these evil volumes from the shelves and keep only those books that have happy endings. Thank you."

Roberta Hokum gave a little bow, and more people clapped. The five selectmen nodded soberly, then asked the head librarian to respond.

Alma had never been very good at public speaking and got nervous whenever she had to stand up in front of a large group of people. Added to this, she hadn't really had a chance to think about what she was going to say, because she had been so busy getting the ghosts out of the books. Ted Parker touched his wife's arm encouragingly as she got to her feet and cleared her throat.

"Thank you for giving me a chance to reply," she said. "I like happy endings too, as much as anybody. Of course, it's nice when everything turns out all right. But as you know, that isn't always the case. Life is full of tragedies. History isn't a cheerful story. Not everything comes up smelling like roses. Books should tell the truth. They shouldn't sugarcoat the facts. If we try to protect our children from all of the depressing things in the world, what are they going to do when they actually go out and face the truth? We should prepare them to understand the difference between right and wrong, not make them think that everything is good. Just because a book describes something ugly or unpleasant doesn't mean it shouldn't be read. A good book can make us laugh, but it can also scare us. It can make us cry or it can make us think, which is the most important thing of all. I'm sure that Mrs. Hokum is concerned about her students, but if we take her advice, there won't be any books left on these shelves.

A library is a place where people are free to read for themselves. And readers should be able to choose their own books, not have others make those choices for them. And certainly, the last thing we need in Carville is for anyone to start burning books. Thank you."

Ted Parker, Orion, Ming, and Courtney clapped loudly as Alma sat down with an uneasy feeling in her chest.

"That was great," whispered Courtney, "but I'm not sure anyone is convinced."

Orion glanced around at the solemn faces of the adults in the room and felt discouraged. The selectmen looked at one another with serious expressions, but before anyone else could speak, Roberta Hokum stood up again.

"She's hiding something!" said the teacher. "There are books in her office that she's trying to keep from us. I'm sure if you look at those books, you'll know what I'm talking about. Those are evil volumes!"

The chairman turned to Alma and asked, "Is that true?"

"No, of course not. Those aren't evil books, and there's nothing to hide," she said. "We can bring them out here and you can take a look for yourselves."

Alma signaled to Orion, Ming, and Courtney. As everyone watched, they carried out the books and stacked them on the table in front of the five selectmen, who began reading the titles and leafing through the pages. The townspeople stood silently, waiting for their reaction, as Roberta Hokum flashed a fluorescent smile of confidence.

After fifteen minutes, the selectmen conferred, huddled behind the stacks of books. Then the chairman stood up and addressed the gathering.

"We understand and appreciate Mrs. Hokum's concerns, especially when it comes to protecting our young people. A public library should be safe and secure, a place where parents can be assured that their children aren't going to be exposed to dangerous influences. However, there is nothing here that seems objectionable. We have unanimously agreed that these books don't pose any threat. The town meeting is adjourned."

Everyone in the room looked at one another in surprise, and Roberta began to shout, "Wait! Wait! You haven't inspected all of them!"

A few people went forward and picked up books. Flipping through the pages, they shook their heads. There was nothing subversive about *Optical Experiments in Nineteenth Century England* or a three-volume first edition of *Anchors Away!: Memoirs of a New England Sea Captain*, or even *Operation Johnny Rook*.

Roberta looked stunned by the sudden verdict. After trying to stop the selectmen from leaving, she rushed down into the stacks. "Wait! There are lots of evil books here. Look, they're all in the basement!" But nobody followed her, and when she switched on the light in the stacks, Roberta found herself alone. She stood there for a moment in her yellow high heels, reaching out as if to grab for something but finding nothing within her reach.

Just then there was a whispering sound, answered by a hushed murmur. From behind a row of metal stacks, Nick Osgood's ghost emerged. A second later, Porquoix appeared, followed by other phantoms, including Sheikh Rustom Ibn Fanous al Ifrit. Roberta looked at them in horror, her eyes opening wide and her lips parting to make a choked sound—as if she had a fishbone caught in her throat. The stacks began to tilt, and for the first time in years, Mrs. Hokum's smile disappeared. Her heels wobbled and her arms went slack. The ceiling leaned and the walls wavered as her knees gave way and she fainted, collapsing to the floor.

40

The Carville World's Fair was held in the cafeteria of the middle school, on the final day of classes. Tables were arranged along the walls, and each group of sixth graders had set up a display. Mrs. Hokum wasn't there, having gone on medical leave for the last week of the semester. She was replaced by Ms. Kinkle, one of the substitute teachers, who had a genuine smile and always spoke to her students in an encouraging voice.

Ms. Kinkle let Orion and Ming finish their report on Ilhas dos Fantasmas. She even allowed Courtney to help them, and their display was judged the best in the World's Fair. (Marigold Deitz had joined a different group.) Their display included three posters, one of which showed a map of the Indian Ocean with the islands clearly visible near the equator, and arrows indicating the flow of the Bromeil current. The second poster depicted the history of the islands, with pictures of the earliest settlers— Prithvi Sangarajan and his wife, Philomenia. It had accounts of shipwrecks and stories of some of the sailors who were washed ashore, including Sheikh Rustom. They also had an exhibit of feather money, with a map showing the migratory patterns of the birds that passed through Prithvideep.

There was a brief note about Hezekiah Osgood, though Orion and Ming decided not to mention any of his experiments. The third poster was about modern Prithvideep, with the dates of independence and a chart of the government, as well as graphs showing economic growth and recent developments in tourism. Ming had e-mailed the embassy of Ilhas dos Fantasmas in Washington, and they had sent a collection of brochures for hotels and beach resorts on Prithvideep.

But the most interesting part of the display was a large starcatcher's scroll made of bark cloth, which Ms. Parker had found in one of the boxes in the library attic, part of the Osgood Collection. The scroll was about four feet long and two feet wide, with an intricate pattern of curved markings that looked as if they had been drawn with a compass. Orion and Ming had borrowed it for the fair, along with the thumb piano. They'd made a sign: PLEASE DO NOT TOUCH, but there wasn't much danger of that. Everyone who walked by their display recoiled as soon as they saw the human skull, then peered at it with curiosity, trying to figure out what the strange instrument was.

Though the three of them had decided not to include any of the arora themselves in their report, they did have a section on mythology and folklore, which included some of the stories of ghosts. One of these was the romance of Nalini and D'Kele, which Courtney had written and illustrated. Orion had also recorded the story of the boy named Tarquin Tao-Jenkins, whom he interviewed about all of his adventures while kidnapped by pirates. Orion had gotten Tarquin to tell his story into a tape recorder and then played it backward so that he could understand what the ghost said. The arora that Ming had befriended, Cziczee, had written a list of all the common names of the birds and plants on Prithvideep, without their Latin equivalents. Along with this she had drawn pictures of some of the more interesting species. Ming had also retrieved the envelope with the stamp from Ilhas dos Fantasmas and added that to their exhibit.

Pinned up behind the display was the national flag of Prithvideep that Orion had copied onto an old pillowcase—most of it was blue with a white circle in the middle that contained an image of the conch shell with wings. Courtney had redone her tattoo, and she had also drawn the same symbol on Orion's and Ming's cheeks.

All morning, parents and other visitors filed past the display and asked questions. Nobody had ever heard of this country before. Courtney's mother visited their booth, as well as Ming's and Orion's parents. Even Enoch Knox came by, dressed in his black suit. When he saw the skull, he looked puzzled for a moment, as if he were trying to recognize who it was. Stroking his moustache, he nodded solemnly at the three friends, then gave them a conspiratorial wink, as if he knew that they had sneaked into his funeral home.

Just as the World's Fair was about to close, Alma and Ted Parker arrived. Hurrying through the doors of the cafeteria, they went straight across to Orion and Ming's table to congratulate them on winning first prize.

"I only wish that Nick and the others could see your display," said Alma. "But I don't think it would be a good idea if they showed up."

"Are they still in the library?"

"Yes," said Alma, picking up one of the travel brochures, which had pictures of thatched cottages surrounding a tropical lagoon. "So far we've been able to keep them hidden, but the sooner we get them out of there the better."

"What are you going to do?"

Alma looked at Ted and smiled.

"We're going on a vacation," he said. "I think we deserve a break after all we've been through."

Orion and the others looked surprised.

"Where are you going?"

Ted Parker pointed to the map in their display.

"We've decided to visit Ilhas dos Fantasmas," said Alma, opening a leaflet with pictures of coconut trees and coral reefs. "I'm curious to see what Prithvideep is really like, and I could use a few weeks on the beach, with plenty of good books to read."

"That's great," said Courtney. "When do you leave?"

"We're flying tomorrow," said Ted. "Right after I hand in my chemistry grades."

"Thanks for your help, all three of you," said Alma. "I promise to send you postcards."

Now that the anxiety and confusion of the past few days had ended, it felt strange not to be rushing about the library and searching through the stacks. There was an awkward pause, and nobody seemed to know what to say, though Alma looked as if she had a secret she wanted to share with them.

Ming was the first to realize what was going on.

"Have you packed already?" she asked, with a knowing grin.

"Not quite," said Alma, nodding. "We've still got a few ghosts to fit in our suitcases."

As soon as she said this, Orion and Courtney understood what was happening too. The arora would soon be returning home! Reunited after years in exile, Nalini and D'Kele would walk hand in hand along the beaches of Prithvideep, leaving no footprints in the sand. Once again, Ilhas dos Fantasmas would be populated by phantoms—Cziczee, Tarquin, Sheikh Rustom, Porquoix . . .

"What about Nick?" asked Courtney.

"He's coming with us too," said Alma. "There's no way he'd let us leave him behind."

Ming glanced up at the star-catcher's scroll, which was part of their display. She couldn't help but wonder if all of this was written in the curved patterns printed on the rough bark cloth.

Lla retfa gindne yppah a eb dluow ereht ebyam.